AFRAID TO DEATH

Marc Behm

DOVER PUBLICATIONS, INC.
Mineola, New York

Copyright

Copyright © 1991 by Marc Behm
All rights reserved.

Bibliographical Note

This Dover edition, first published in 2019, is an unabridged republication of the work originally printed by No Exit Press, Harpenden, England, in 2000.

Library of Congress Cataloging-in-Publication Data

Names: Behm, Marc, author.
Title: Afraid to death / Marc Behm.
Description: Mineola, New York : Dover Publications, Inc., 2019. | "This Dover edition, first published in 2019, is an unabridged republication of the work originally printed by No Exit Press, Harpenden, England, in 2000."
Identifiers: LCCN 2018039370| ISBN 9780486827575 | ISBN 0486827577
Subjects: LCSH: Antiheroes—Fiction.
Classification: LCC PS3552.E38 A69 2019 | DDC 813/.54—dc23
LC record available at https://lccn.loc.gov/2018039370

Manufactured in the United States by LSC Communications
82757701 2019
www.doverpublications.com

Life was brought to us by some unknown force; we don't know where it came from, or why …

Solzhenitsyn

1

He never knew when she was coming, that's why he had to pay close attention to all the omens. Otherwise she would take him by surprise.

This morning, for instance, in Indianapolis.

He was playing cards all night with Maxie Hearn and two guys who made TV commercials. They were in Maxie's penthouse on top of a building on English Avenue. He won twenty-six thousand dollars.

The sun was rising when he showed them his last hand. A king, two aces and two eights.

'Hey!' Maxie said. 'Bad news!'

'What?'

'A pair of eights and a pair of aces. You know what that means?'

'No.'

'They call it a deadman's hand.'

That was all the warning he needed. He got out of there. Fast.

He got off the elevator on the third floor and went down the service stairs to the back exit. He was trembling, sweaty, his lips were chalky, there were black dots swirling all over the walls. The old familiar symptoms of pure funk.

He cut through an alley, hid behind a tree.

She was there!

Sitting on a bench on English Avenue, watching the apartment entranceway.

He ran back through the alley to Prospect Street.

He didn't bother to go to his hotel. There was nothing there worth keeping. Christ! How many neckties had he left behind in how many hotel rooms in how many cities? How many books, cigars, jackets, extra pairs of shoes, toothbrushes ...?

He had a getaway valise in a locker at the bus terminal. He took a Greyhound to Lebanon, another to Crawfordville, another to Lafayette.

Once, years and years ago, he'd written a song about his many narrow escapes.

Ho! ho! ho! ho!
Just go Joe go go go!
She'll get you if you go too slow!

Not much of a song. Not much to *ho! ho!* about. But it was better than a requiem.

It was raining in Lafayette.

That night he flew to San Francisco. She wasn't on the plane, thank God!

2

Joe met her for the first time when he was eleven years old. On Greenwood Avenue.

That was the year they bought the big house by the lake. His father was a professor of Musicology at the University. He was writing a book on Brahms. Mom worked for Hillcrest Realtors. She drove a scarlet Ferrari 328 GTS.

Joe bought an old canoe for eighteen dollars. The guy at the boatyard said it was a genuine Seneca imitation. He'd paddle it across the lake every morning to Dire Point and leave it there under the wharf of one of the summer cottages. Then he'd walk to school, past the chapel and the country club and along Greenwood Avenue to Washington Boulevard.

This morning she was in the middle of the block, standing under a tree beside a mailbox. She was blond, wearing a black raincoat, black boots and a black beret.

She smiled at him. They were all alone on the long, green, sunny avenue, just the two of them.

She had purple eyes.

'Good morning,' she said in a voice from Somewhere Else. Maybe South America. Or Asia. Or Canada.

'What's your name?'

'Joe Egan.'

'You're Professor Egan's son?'

'Yes, ma'am.'

Enormous eyes! He could see himself reflected in the purple.

'I heard him conduct Brahms' *Ein Deutsches Requiem* last year at Yale. It was magnificent.'

'I know all the words by heart.'

'You do? All of them? Do you speak German?'

'Nope. I learnt the phonetics.'

'Denn dies Fleisch est ist wie Cras,' she sang softly, *'und alle herrlichkeit wie des Grases Blumen.'*

'Das Gras is verdorret,' he sang, *'und die blume abgefallen.'*

'Do you know what it means?'

'Nope.'

'"Behold, all flesh is as grass … and lo the grass withers and the flower decays."' She stared at him, drowning him in her eyes. Eyes like the lake, like the sky in the lake. 'Where does Mr. Morgan live, Joe?' Like the sun, deep deep in the lake.

'Over there,' he pointed to Morgan's house. 'He's sick.'

'Yes, I am aware of that. Thank you. I'll see you around.'

She crossed the street, humming the *Requiem.*

Coming back from school that afternoon at four o'clock, he saw a wreath on the front door of Morgan's house.

3

'Morgan died this morning,' Mom said.

His father was shocked. 'But I thought he was up and around! I saw him in his back yard yesterday! He was hanging laundry on the god-damn clothesline!'

'According to Peggy-Sue, he was watching television when somebody rang the doorbell. And he just slumped to the floor. Bingo.'

Mr. Morgan was a riding instructor at the Equestrian Academy. He fell off his horse in the woods last month and broke something. Everybody said he was drunk.

'Who rang the doorbell?' Joe asked.

'I don't know.'

He thought about it all that sleepless night and most of the next day and finally decided that he was just being spooky. Mr. Morgan's death and the blond girl's purple eyes and the *Requiem* were nothing but what Dad called contrapuntal. 'Communism and Nazism are contrapuntal,' he'd say. 'Just like Laurel and Hardy.' Joe wasn't sure what he was talking about, but he loved the word and used it whenever he had a chance.

A week later he was plunged into a new book, *How to Play Bridge,* and forgot all about it.

Bridge was almost as impossible as algebra. He decided to memorize the book from cover to cover. It took him a year to master all the rules and diagrams. By the time he was thirteen he was an honorary member of Mom's Thursday afternoon bridge club. And along the way he picked up canasta, gin rummy, cribbage and pinocle.

Dad taught him how to play poker.

Then she came back.

It was on Valentine's Day. He paddled his Seneca canoe all the way to the Isle on the lake's far western end.

The Isle was a dismal place, filled with dangerous bogs and watersnakes lying on logs. But on a humpback in its center was a square of broken stone columns and paved paths going nowhere. And a sundial on a pedestal. And a granite slab!

Ugh!

He was sure that long ago, even before Time, little boys and girls were sacrificed here. Warlocks in masks chopped them up with hatchets and pulled out their livers and fed them to the snakes. He called it the Temple of Cadenza. (That was another of Dad's favorite words; he was always raving about Wilhelm Kempff's and Robert Casadesus' cadenzas.) But the truth of the matter was that Cadenza was a merciless subterranean god, bloodier than Dracula, who devoured kids' bones when they were still *alive.* And backwards his name spelled *aznedac,* which, in the Ancient Language, meant 'split down the middle.'

He'd only been here once before. That had been when he discovered Benton, the history professor, blowing a quarterback named Speed Evans.

Joe made up his mind once and for all – when he was about ten – that he was a DOS. Discoverer of Secrets. It was a gift, like ESR. You either had to keep your cool and accept it, or fuck all.

Rule No. 1: DTN. Don't Tell Nobody.

He never blabbed about Benton and Speed Evans. Then he found out that owlfaced old Madam Manner, the General's widow, snorted coke. Her chauffeur, Nat, bought the stuff for her from a pusher in one of the frat houses. He never mentioned that to anyone either. He also knew that Professor Jarvis's wife, Lil, was making it with a fireman in East Elm. And that Dr. Robert's nurse and Morgan's niece, Peggy-Sue ditto. And that Dr. Robert and the same nurse ditto. And that Nellie Jarman, the Dean's daughter, stole nailpolish from the drugstore and Shakespeare albums from the record shop.

He knew something else about Nellie too, so Top Secret it was sacred. One afternoon, while Maurice Evans recited Hamlet's soliloquies on her phono, they'd taken off all their clothes and examined each other's nakedness. She had been astounded to discover that *it* looked like a pencil and he'd been just as impressed by her lacking one. She'd made him kiss her there, then cried and let him rub against her. Wow! That had been super-nifty! They'd eaten a whole box of Mr. Goodbars she'd stolen from the market that afternoon. After that they used to meet in a boathouse on Dire Cove. He taught her how to play poker.

Mom and Dad didn't know anything about these goings on. They were as innocent as Hansel and Gretel.

Anyway …

There was nothing happening on the Isle today. He ate a couple of apples and cleaned the sundial and pulled weeds and vines out of the pathways. He read 'The Raven' by Edgar Allen Poe, then memorized it. He carved his initials on a column: JE. He was named after his Uncle Joe, who'd been a fighter pilot with the 8th Air Force in WW2. His Lightning was shot down over Metz in 1944.

That was another secret he was a Discoverer Of. Miss Emma, the head librarian, told him that Uncle Joe was the father of her son, Nat. She made him swear not to repeat this fact to a living soul.

So Nat was his cousin. And Mom's nephew. And Madam Manner's chauffeur. Ha ha! Who would believe that?

At four o'clock he paddled back across the lake.

And he saw her!

She was standing on the shore of the inlet behind the house, throwing pebbles in the water. All in black. With a black scarf tied around her bright blond hair.

She waved to him.

He steered the canoe into the rushes under the heavy willows. Nobody could get him there. He waited an hour. When he came ashore she was gone.

Madam Manners and Lil Jarvis were whispering on the front porch. Professor Jarvis was in the living room, telephoning.

His father was sitting in the kitchen, sobbing like a madman.

'Mom, Joe ... Mom ...' he was making awful noises. 'Her Ferrari went into the river ...'

4

By Christmas Dad had stopped sobbing. He conducted a New Year's concert at Harvard and that summer finished his book on Brahms. He moved out of the bedroom into the guest room. Then he began meeting one of his students in a motel in Cooperstown.

Nobody knew this but Joe, thanks to his DOS talents. But he didn't give a rat's ass. He had other things to think about – studying maps, charting an escape route, preparing hiding places, saving his money, doing push-ups to keep in shape.

If she came again, he knew exactly what he was going to do. His knapsack was ready, packed with provisions. He'd take the canoe over to the lake's western end, not to the Isle … oh, no! She'd expect him to stay there, hiding like a cornered rat. She'd come ashore, laughing at him. *Joe! Come out come out wherever you are!* No way! He'd just keep going, paddling into the mouth of the river, then on upstream deep in the woods. He'd spend the night there, sleeping in a tree. The next day he'd hike cross-country, quick-time, to Fairoaks … not to South Fairoaks, oh, no, which was closest, but to North Fairoaks, two miles farther on. But then she'd be searching the woods for him, gibbering with rage, looking for his spoor. But he'd be long gone. At Fairoaks, he'd catch a local train to Kentville and …

Yeah, then what?

He couldn't figure out where to go next. Not that it mattered. He'd play it by ear. Wander around for a week or so, lying low. Then come home. She couldn't hang around here forever. She had a busy schedule and had to keep moving on. No? She'd probably just put him on the back burner for a while. And by the time she showed up again, he'd have something else worked out. The main thing was to keep dodging her.

Yeah. But how long could he do that? What a fucking nightmare!

'What's the matter with you?' Dad asked. 'You're always mumbling to yourself. And why do you keep looking out the window? She won't come back.'

Joe jumped. What did he mean by that? 'Who?' Did he know something? 'Who won't be coming back?'

'Mom.'

'Oh.'

'Remember what Claudius told Hamlet. "Your mother lost a mother and that mother lost hers. Obsequious sorrow is obstinate stubbornness."'

'Hamlet didn't lose his mother.'

'C'est égal. His mother and father were contrapuntal. I want you to have a talk with Father Patrick. Maybe he can do something for you. Help you to get through this ordeal.'

So Joe began going to Mass every Sunday.

Then came the clipboard caper.

As usual, Dad was in Cooperstown, shaking up with his girlfriend. (Another DOS bit: she was making it on the side with a senior named – ugh! – Porky.) It was raining. Joe couldn't sleep.

He decided to jerk off. There was a recent photo of Catherine Deneuve in *Life* magazine. Just her face. But that was enough. His imagination could invent the rest of her. She was his favorite actress. He rented all her cassettes – *Belle de jour* – wow! Just watching her and listening to her was like yike! What a goddess!

He gazed at her and pulled out his dong. But he couldn't get it up. She wasn't the same. Nope. Her nose was different … and her cheeks … Maybe she'd had a lift job.

Besides, he didn't feel like it.

He drank what was left in a bottle of Black Label. His father often did that and always ended up snoring.

Yeah, everything had changed. The lake used to be beautiful. Now it was a cold purple tomb. Ferraris had turned ugly. He was afraid to walk along Greenwood Avenue. Now he took the bus to school, like a nerd in a TV movie. And his dong was shriveled up. Catherine Deneuve was somebody else. And the nights were scary … scary … scary …

The next thing he knew he was on the campus, vomiting and rolling in the grass. They put him in an ambulance and took him to the kids' hospital in Cooperstown.

They pumped out his guts and dumped him in a ward with a dozen other teens. One guy's legs were hanging on ropes. Another had tubes sticking out of his mouth, as if he'd swallowed an octopus. The shithead in the bed next to him was wrapped in bandages like *The Curse of the Mummy.*

What a festival of basketcases! It was worse than a sacrifice to Candenza.

But misery brought him a hiatus of peace and he finally slept.

He woke at dawn. Beside him, the Mummy was wheezing loudly. He sounded like a clarinet. What was he saying? *Lookout lookout lookout...*

She was there!

He saw her the moment his eyes opened, standing in the gray haze at the far end of the ward.

His escape plans collapsed in ruins and he just gaped at her. She walked to the first bed in the row and read the name on the clipboard.

He slipped out from under the covers, dropped to the floor, moved cautiously to the foot of his bed. He unhooked his clipboard, carried it over to the Mummy's bed. He didn't believe for one minute that he'd get away, but he couldn't think of anything else to do. She had him in a dead-end and there was nowhere to run.

She was in the middle of the ward now, reading all the names.

He took down the Mummy's board, hung his own in its place. He brought the other board back to his bed, hooked it up, then slid quickly under the covers.

His ears were buzzing. A whole beehive of bright white dots was flying around his head. He prayed. *Hail,*

Holy Queen, Mother of Mercy, our life and our hope. To thee we cry, poor banished children of Eve ...

Play dead ... fake it ... don't move ... he was Lieutenant Joe Egan, Troop C. 117 Cavalry ... he'd ridden into an ambush in Cooperstown Canyon ... all his troopers were lying around him deader than shit ... the Apaches were prowling through the corpses to see if any of them were still alive to tortue, torter ... tort ... torture ... fake it ... fake it ...

She was two beds away, reading the Leg's name ... then the Octopus Swallower's ... now his ... *to thee we send up our sighs, mourning and weeping in this valley of tears ...*

He closed his eyes. He was twitching like a junkie, his fingers were itchy ... *benedictus et sanctus ... Father Almighty ... Deo Deo Deo ...*

He opened one eye.

She was bending over the Mummy, touching his bandages, whispering to him.

Then it was over. He couldn't believe it. She was gone! Somewhere in the hospital a bell was ringing. Ding ding ding hah ding ding hah hah ...

She had actually come and gone without seeing him. And he was lying there, right under her nose! Jesus! What luck! Going to Mass every Sunday had really paid off. God was really and truly a neat dude. Yeah! But ...

The Mummy had stopped wheezing.

5

'It seems to me you tricked her very cunningly,' Father Patrick said. Not many boys could have reacted that cleverly … uhh … under similar circumstances … uhh … They tell me you left the hospital before you were supposed to.'

'Yeah. To play safe, I split out through the basement.'

'Where did you go? Your dad was frantic.'

'To the library. It was Sunday, but I know how to break in. The lock on the skylight is broken. I hid in stacks all day and read *August 1914* by Alexander Solhitsyn.'

'Solzhenitsyn.'

'Whatever.'

They were sitting in the orchard behind the chapel. This was the first time he'd ever discussed the blonde with anyone. It was easy, talking to Father Patrick. He was always cool. You could tell him anything, no matter how far-out, and he'd just puff on his cigar and say, 'Uhh'.

Joe watched the boats on the lake. That's how the Mummy got hurt. A Yamaha Flyer ran over him, right down there off Dire Point.

'Did I kill him, Father?'

'Nonsense. You didn't kill anybody.'

'No … but … like …'

'He was killed in the water. Swimming. When they brought him to the hospital, Dr. Roberts said he wouldn't last the night. You weren't in any way responsible for that.

'Uhh … look, Joe,' he relit his smelly cigar. 'Even if you're right, if this woman is really … uhh … who you think she is … I'm not saying she isn't … but I have to admit, I have my doubts.'

'That's okay. As long as you half-believe me at least.'

'Well, if she is, would she be that easy to fool? Just by changing the clipboards on the beds? What I mean is, if she wanted to find you, don't you suppose she could? Easily.'

'Maybe not, Father. No. I figure she has so much to do that she just can't keep track of everybody. If I just stay on the move, she'll never catch me.'

'I see.'

'It's a question of out-guessing her.'

'But you can't keep running away forever. There's no future in that.'

'But I have to!' Just thinking about it made him jittery. The orchard was beginning to close in on him. The hillside sloping down to the lake was another dead-end. And the chapel's stained-glass windows seemed to be on fire. 'I have to keep watching for her and I have to be ready to *move.* Fast.'

'But you're going to work yourself into a continuous frenzy and end up having a massive stroke.'

'Yeah right. I have to remember to keep laid back.'

'And no more boozing.'

'No way Jose. Ugh!'

Father Patrick smoked his cigar and Joe tried to keep his eyes open. Every time he closed them he saw her in the ward. Shit! He had to admit though that it was peaceful here. He could probably take a quick nap. Or maybe he could become a priest. No ... that would mean being locked up in some monastery with bars on the windows, like a slammer. Like a hospital. Like the Isle. Like everything.

'Listen to me, Joe. Pay attention now.'

'Right.'

'It's not a question of whether or not I believe you.'

'What's important is that you believe me.'

'Right.'

'You'll see her again.'

'Oh, balls! No!'

'Wait. You'll see her again, sure. But not for a long long time. She knows you're waiting for her. That puts her at a great disadvantage, you see, your being aware of her presence.'

'Yeah, that makes sense.' It did. Like that book on Gettysburg he'd read twice. The Army of Northern Virginia was at a disadvantage and lost the battle. Because the Army of the Potomac knew where the next attack was coming from. Not on the left flank or the right flank but right to the center. Pickett's charge. A disaster. The old priest was thinking straight, like he always did. Cool reasoning.

'So she'll just wait until your guard is down. Years and years will pass before she makes her move. That will give you a whole … uhh … lifetime to think about something else.'

'A whole lifetime?'

'Uhh … practically'

He was right.

The years passed like andantes. Only strangers died. Joe graduated from college. Dad married his girlfriend and they sold the house and moved to London.

Joe went to work for the Esor Tobacco Labs in Raleigh, North Carolina. He came back to the lake only once, to paddle over to the Isle one last time. And to say goodbye to Father Patrick. But the Isle was flooded and he couldn't go ashore. And the old priest wasn't as sharp as he used to be and didn't even recognize him.

Joe walked along Greenwood Avenue, past the chapel and the country club and Morgan's house. He stopped and looked around. Where was it? Here somewhere in the middle of the block.

What's your name?

Joe Egan.

Behold all flesh is as grass and lo the grass withers and the flower decays.

He walked over to the mailbox. *Here.* This is where she'd been standing. Exactly sixteen years ago.

God! Children's minds were more gruesome than Edgar Allan Poe. What would the shrinks have to say about all that juvenile morbidity? They'd probably relate it to the sex urge. And they'd be right. His memory of her was blurred but he did recall very vividly the curves of her hips moving under her raincoat. And her black stockings. And those purple eyes!

The poor woman. Today she'd be a plump elderly yuppie with blue hair, without any inkling whatever of the havoc she'd caused him.

Well, if he couldn't say goodbye to Father Patrick, he'd at least bid her farewell.

Hail and adieu!

6

He rented a large apartment on the third floor of a high rise on Peace Street. An incredible place, four rooms and two baths, for only five hundred a month. He drove to work, in New Hope, every morning at nine and was home by eight-thirty On Friday nights he'd try to cruise, but there wasn't much action in Raleigh. Everyone – except the couples – was terrified of AIDS. In fact, so was he. So most of his efforts to pick up girls were half-hearted. It was mostly concerts and parties and dinners and tennis, with even the necking reduced to an absolute minimum. There was a lot of snorting going on, but he avoided that.

It never occurred to him that it was a dull life. He was comfortable, just vegetating and prowling around. Even the boring routine at Esor was bearable. Computers were always fascinating. And his co-workers weren't all assholes.

But his greatest pleasure, the thing that filled most of his voids, was poker. There was a game somewhere almost every night and the pots were stupendous – at first terrifying, but gradually luring him like beckoning sirens. Some weekends he'd go all the way to Goldsboro or Rocky Mount for big all-night sessions. Within less than two years he had thirty grand in his savings account. He bought a BMW.

So all was well.

But he was dying for a friendly blow-job.

Then he met Ada.

She worked in the financial department. She had short hair and green eyes. They looked at each other one afternoon in the cafeteria and both saw something so compelling that they had to sit at the same table.

It was from her that he learned that he was well known in all the departments as a champion card player. Everybody had a different estimate of how much he'd won – some claimed it was over a million dollars. He was astonished. He had no idea that he was a celebrity.

They went to a basketball game that night and the next to the theatre to see *Coriolanus*. The third evening they got slightly poleaxed on bourbon, but not enough to go to bed. That was out of the question. But they discussed it.

'I'm clean,' Ada admitted.

'Me too.'

'How can *either* of us be sure though?'

'Exactly.'

'Maybe the last girl you slept with slept with someone else who slept with someone else and so on all the way back to Peter the Positive.'

'There you are.'

'It's just too risky. I mean, hey! It's a plague. Even with those awful ski-masks you guys put on your tools. They make penises look like KKK Grand Dragons.'

'Have you ever used a vibrator?'

'I'd be afraid of electrocuting myself. What do you do to relieve yourself?'

'Poker. No pun intended. My lust is sublimated.'

'Speaking of poker, aren't we a sorry pair of jokers?'

She went home alone. So did he.

She was twenty-eight years old, originally from Oklahoma City. She'd been with Esor for five years and was in charge of payrolls.

Before Joe, she'd been going out with a lawyer from the legal department. 'Paul and I never had coitus either,' she told him. 'We decided to date simply as a career move. We didn't want the Powers That Be to think we were gay. Well, I did play with him a couple of times. Wearing a rubber glove dipped in suntan lotion. But we stopped that, it was too painful. Then he got hooked on crack and showed up at the office one morning in his pajamas. They carried him away in a strait-jacket. You can imagine what that did to my reputation. Career move indeed! The Board of Directors actually had me investigated. Honestly! A private eye was following me around for months.'

She'd always planned to marry and have a child before she was thirty, but the Big Scare disrupted the scheme. 'Living a normal life,' she said, 'has become as difficult as running for President of the United States. My entire life is a god-damned sham. Six hours a day at Esor, watching the clock, and the rest of the time total vacuity. My salary has doubled since last year, but so what! If I can't even get laid once in a while, what's the point? That's why I cut my hair. I'm a nun. Aside from poor Paul, you're the first guy I've even talked to intimately since college.'

But things weren't as desperate as all that. She knew a nurse who worked at Rex Hospital and one Sunday she gave them both an AIDS test. On Monday a.m. they were pronounced pure. On Monday p.m. they took a shower together and had their first soaring orgasms on the bathroom floor.

So now they were a couple.

They made up for lost time with rabbit-like zeal – at her place, at his, in his office, in hers, in parking lots, in elevators, in closets, on tennis courts.

They married that summer. They went to London on their honeymoon to visit his father and Mom II. They found Dad living in a drab flat with a black violinist from Haiti. Mom II had run off to Madrid with a lover.

Dad was overjoyed to see them. He confessed that he was broke. He wanted them both to quit their jobs and stay in England. Joe could support them all – including the violinist – by playing poker.

Joe gave him ten thousand dollars and whisked his bride off to Venice and Rome.

When they returned to Raleigh Ada gave up her studio in Millbrook and moved into his apartment on Peace Street.

All that January Raleigh was buried in snow. Esor closed down at noon and by three o'clock the streets were as dark as the Yukon. That afternoon – the 17th, Joe remembered – Ada was already home when he came stumbling in, soggy and frozen. He stripped and stretched out in front of the blazing fireplace. When she saw him, lying there, bare-assed and shivering, events took their usual turn.

'Let's pretend we're horny sailors on a whaling ship,' she suggested. 'Locked in the ice of the Arctic Ocean. You haven't seen a woman since you left Nantucket. And I'm that cute little cabin-boy who's been flirting with you since the beginning of the voyage.'

'I can't wait to shout, "That she blows."'

'If you do, it's all over between us.'

'How about, "Spouting to starboard!"'

'How about just shutting up? If the Captain finds us down here in the hold like this, he'll put us in irons.'

'Do I at least get to toss my harpoon?'

'Aye! Aye! But first, I'll thaw you out.'

Afterwards, she reminded him that they were supposed to go to a party tonight. They considered calling it off, but it was only a block away, on Oberlin Road, so they decided to go.

'Oh, I almost forgot,' she said. 'You had a phone call.'

'Who was it?'

'Some woman.'

'Christ, I really don't feel like facing the elements, it's ninety-below out there.'

'We'll leave early. You can wear one of your Italian neckties.'

'It was probably Miss Suffolk's secretary. About my vouchers.'

'She wouldn't give me her name. In fact, it was very suspicious. You're not thawing out with some other broad, are you?'

'You flatter me. Who do you think I am, Hercules?'

She reached for him. 'Sure. I bet I can get it up again in ten seconds.'

She was right. But suddenly her fingers turned to ice and he lost it. 'A woman? You're sure it was a woman?'

'I know the difference between a man and a woman, even though I am a cabin-boy of doubtful gender.'

'What did she say?'

'Hey!' she bent over him. 'Where did it go?'

'What did she say, Ada?'

'That she'd see you later.'

7

Even a blizzard couldn't keep people away from one of Stan and Mabel Stokowski's potluck soirées. The food was always fabulous. There were fifty guests crowded around the buffet when Ada and Joe arrived.

'Hold me back,' she whispered. 'Caviar! And pâté de campagne! And a salade niçoise! I'm going to help myself before these hungry hogs devour everything.'

And she disappeared into the mob.

Joe leaned against a wall and tried to bring his jerking muscles under control. Who could have called? It must have been one of the girls who played poker … Charlotte or Mona or Michele or Carrie or … But why wouldn't she leave her name? Or it could have been somebody from the bank. Or, for that matter, just someone selling subscriptions or something. And what about an overseas call? London. Mom II or Dad's violinist. Or somebody they'd met in Italy? Or a friend of a friend …

Anyway, there was no reason to get frantic about it. That way lay madness!

'I think it's revolting.'

He jumped. One of his bosses, Miss Suffolk, was glaring at him.

'Are you referring to my necktie, Miss Suffolk?'

'No, your tie is very pretty.'

'I bought sixteen of them in Rome. On my honeymoon.'

'You look livid. Are you drunk?'

'I don't drink.'

'Good. A boozer is always a loser.'

She ought to know. She kept a bottle of Johnny Walker in her desk and by four o'clock every afternoon called computers 'compooters' and programs 'pogroms.' According to rumor, she owned 51 percent of Esor.

'Look at him,' she hissed. 'Smirking and simpering like the lord of the manor. Pride cometh before the fall.'

What the fuck was she talking about. 'Who?'

'Tony Waterman. The insipid cockroach. He shouldn't be here, showing off like that.'

'Why not, Miss Suffolk?'

Tony Waterman was in charge of the personnel department. He wore Miama Vice outfits, even in midwinter, and smoked grass in public. Ada called him Stony Tony.

'Because it just isn't gentlemanly behavior, that's why not.'

'I don't understand.'

'He happens to be banging Mabel Stokowski. Don't tell me you didn't know that.'

'Nope.'

'I'm not surprised. If you want to succeed you must take heed.'

'I beg your pardon …'

'You won't climb the ladder in this corporation,

young man, if you aren't aware of what's going on around you. Let me remind you, Joe, that you haven't been promoted, not once, in two years. The heedful are never needful.'

'Yeah right, but if one to the grindstone keeps his nose, one never has time to take off his clothes.'

'Poor Stan is heartbroken.'

'Because I haven't been promoted?'

'No, you ass, because that smug fink is balling his wife.'

After ransacking the buffet, the guests converged on a boy rapping on an xylophone, accompanying a girl in overalls singing Yugoslavian folksongs.

Joe found himself standing next to Mabel Stokowski.

'I phoned you this afternoon,' she whispered.

An enormous flood of relief washed over him. 'Oh, that was you. I was wondering …'

'I want to borrow three hundred dollars.'

'Okay.'

'Stan won't give me any money, the tight-ass bastard. He told the bank not to accept my checks. But that's only *one* of the reasons I loath him. Do you want to know the other reason?'

'Sure.'

'Cunnilingus disgusts him.'

'Oh. Well … listen, Mabel, I'm sorry I wasn't home. But why didn't you just ask Ada?'

'She wasn't home either.'

'No?' his stomach heaved. 'She wasn't? Then who answered the phone?'

'Nobody?'

He pulled open a window. He refused to panic. Fuck that! The wind stung his eyes. It was beginning again, after all these years ... but he wouldn't panic. He took a deep breath of freezing air. It was just a question of thinking clearly and holding funk at bay. Blue funk. Cold blue funk. Keep her at bay too. *Her.* Jesus! He mustn't let her into his thoughts. Keep out!

It was a simple telephone call. Okay. It must have been Michele, in Kenly. The last time he'd seen her she promised to get in touch with him as soon as she had another big game lined up. Right. Michele. Or hey! Wait! That Japanese girl at the garage, about the BMW's brakes. He told her he'd call her back and never did. He'd forgotten all about her. Sure. This was grotesque! He was falling apart for nothing.

Somebody shouted, 'Close the window, numbnuts!'

Michele ... the garage ... who else? The old lady at the bookstore. He'd ordered *I Rode with Stonewall* and *Stonewall in the Valley* and *Sherman's Civil War* from her. She said it would only take a week or so to receive all three books.

Friday Thursday Wednesday Tuesday Monday ... five days ago ...

He closed the window.

Why wouldn't she leave her name?

'Huh what?' One of Ada's accountants lurched past him. A lout named Dudley, goggle-eyed with booze. 'You talking to me, Egan?'

'Hullo, Dudley.'

'Hullo.' He reeled away.

And suddenly she was there.

She came out of the dining room and strolled over to the fireplace with the guests crowded around the xylophone player and the singer.

Joe watched her, too stupefied to move. She was as blond and supple as she'd been on Greenwood Avenue. That was the first thing that stunned him. She hadn't aged or changed. Not in the least.

How was that possible!

She saw him, smiled and nodded to him.

Then a shot was fired and everybody was screaming and stampeding through the rooms.

8

He didn't know how he got out of there. He found himself on Oberlin Road, standing in the snow, pulling on a sheepskin coat that wasn't his. Where was Ada? And where had he parked the car?

He ran toward Peace Street. The bank ... he had to get his money out of his savings account. But he couldn't ... not before Monday ... tomorrow was Saturday ... he couldn't wait that long.

He had to leave *now.* He had his credit cards and some cash. He had to pack. He slid on the ice, banged into a phone booth. No ... he couldn't go back to the apartment! Not away up there on the third floor ... a perfect trap! But he had to pack ... he needed some clothes ... he couldn't leave without luggage ... fuck it! No luggage! He was sliding all over the street, like an ice-skater. He leaned against a mailbox and tried to be – what was the word? – coherent. Okay. (1) He had to get out of Raleigh tonight. (2) No time to pack. (3) Keep away from the apartment. (4) He needed the car. (5) Ada. Oh, God! Ada! He couldn't take her with him. That hit him like a sledgehammer. Ask her to run away with him? She'd think he was insane. And he was! This was as good a time as any to face that fact. He was crazier than a loon!

He waited for her in the underground garage, hiding behind the parked cars. It was after midnight when the BMW rolled down the ramp, its wipers slashing like fencers.

'Where the hell did you disappear to?' She hugged him, her face shining with excitement.

'Something came up, Ada. I have to ...'

'Stan Stokowski shot Stony Tony! He caught him getting on Mabel in the kitchen and shot him!'

'Listen, I have to leave town for a while ...'

'Where did you get that coat?'

'I have to ...'

'Where's your anorak?'

'I must have left it at ...'

'Leave town? What are you talking about?'

'I'll only be gone a couple of days ...' A fucking lie! 'A week at the most.'

'You've been gambling again.'

'Yeah.'

'Who's after you? Bookies?'

'Something like that.'

'Just pay whatever you owe them.'

'I will. Monday. Goodbye, Ada.'

'Wait a second ...'

'I'll be back ...' He kissed her – a cold terrified kiss – then climbed in the car and drove off.

'Joe!'

He'd never forget her calling his name like that. Never. She shouted at him in a thousand night-mares, over and over again.

He did come back. Ten years later.

9

Route 70 to Durham was snowed under. So was 40. He fled in the opposite direction, back across the city to Carleigh. All the exits were blocked. He spent the night in a motel. He didn't sleep. He sat bleakly on the edge of the bed, watching TV and urinating every fifteen minutes.

At dawn he followed a slow-moving snowplow to Goldsboro. From here the road was clear to Kinston. By midnight he was on the coast, in Moreland City. Another motel. He found a clip of six one-hundred dollar bills in the pocket of the sheepskin. A positive omen if ever there was one! But he still couldn't sleep.

One more night, one more motel in South Carolina, then he was in Atlanta.

He decided he'd come far enough. He checked into the New Forest Park, near the airport, and slept for eleven hours.

He swam in the pool, ate huge meals, bought some clothes, took long walks, jogged. An old bell captain gave him an address in East Point and he began playing poker again. But he couldn't concentrate and in two weeks lost most of his cash.

He was paying for everything with checks and credit cards. That meant that all his spending could be traced back to him here in Georgia, but there was no way to avoid that. He'd move on soon enough. To Vegas maybe, or LA.

Eventually. But not until he calmed down.

Then, roaming around one night, he was mugged and lost everything. He didn't report it to the police. The paperwork would just mean further identification. But he cancelled his cards by phone. He was still tidy-minded enough to do that.

At the end of the month he left the hotel without paying his bill. He slept in the BMW.

He got a job waiting on tables in a restaurant on Ivy Street. The tips were generous and he moved into a rooming house. He played some more poker. He kept losing. Then he was fired.

He worked for a while in a carwash, then a supermarket, then in the cafeteria at Spelman College. Then nothing.

A student bought his sheepskin coat for twenty dollars.

He sold the BMW.

More poker, but the losing streak continued. It was definitely hoodoo time.

On his first night on the streets he climbed up on the roof of a service station and slept there. After that, roofs became his specialty – warehouses, office buildings, department stores, schools, the post office, even Exhibition Mall and the St. Joseph Infirmary.

His fellow-derelicts called him 'Housetop Harry' and began imitating him. Soon the roofs of Atlanta were crowded with squatters. The scandal became nationwide and the Mayor ordered the Police Department to put a stop to it. Joe and hundreds of others were herded into the slammer. He gave a false name and was released the next day.

He moved into a large wooden packing case in a vacant lot on Memorial Drive. It was five feet high and seven feet long. He filled it with straw and a mattress and pillows – whatever he could salvage from dumpsters.

He lived there all spring and summer and fall, begging for handouts during the day, entombed as snugly as a bear in a cave at night.

Nobody bothered him, except, occasionally, some neighborhood kids who threw rocks at his hovel and once, when he was out bumming, poured paint on his blankets.

Two black cops visited him and beat him up because he was a honky, but they didn't evict him.

After that he was left alone and became part of the rubble.

10

He'd lie in his decaying hole for hours on end, eating apples and watching the adjacent streets through peepholes.

On the edge of the lot was a bus stop. Farther on, up the block on the corner, was a barbershop. Down the block, on the next corner, were a dry-cleaners and a 7-Eleven. And just across the Drive was the playing field of a school, usually swarming with screeching little girls high-jumping and racing and kicking soccer balls.

His ancient Discoverer of Secrets gift came into use again.

He learned that the wife of the man who owned the dry-cleaners would sometimes sneak across the lot to the barbershop. The barber would hang a 'Closed' sign on the door for a half-hour, then she would sneak back.

A lad who worked in the 7-Eleven was gay. During his afternoon break he'd bring certain customers into the lot and they would perform in the garbage.

And one of the passengers at the bus stop was a smuggler or a spy or something. He would arrive every morning at six-thirty. Another man, not always the same, would get off the next bus that pulled in. As the two of them passed each other, a small bundle would exchange hands, as swiftly and deftly as a magician's trick.

But most of the time he would just watch the little girls in the field. They were like birds, swooping in endless flight, pouncing and hopping, never still. At first, he could hardly tell one from the other. But then, as the weeks passed, he began to identify them familiarly. One was taller than the others, already a lovely ballerina, soaring to incredible heights over the hurdles. One was too fat, much too fat, her nimbleness was beginning to falter. Another, the fastest, was an Oriental. She could streak around the entire track in less than a minute. Three of them looked exactly alike, they had to be triplets.

And one – the smallest – kept trying over and over again to climb the fence, ripping her sweatshirt, scratching her knees, always failing to reach the top. She was just too tiny to make it. But next year she would outgrow them all and be able to ascend barriers twice as high.

He wished he could tell her this.

The traffic was unending. Buses, fire engines, ambulances, cars, trucks. Their rolling tires were as perpetual as the ocean tides.

That's what woke him late one October night – a change in the tide.

He sat up, peeked through a peephole. A car was parked at the bus stop, its motor running, a spotlight beside the driver's window shining on the lot.

He thought the two sadistic black cops were back … but no. It was smaller than a cruiser and unmarked.

He crawled outside, crept into the weeds.

The beam of the light passed just in front of him, then rose and moved on.

He hid behind a pile of refuse. The beam swept back to him, poured into the bushes, drenching the blackness with pale brilliance … then pulled away.

He scampered across the side street into the barbershop alley, crouched in the shadows.

The light found the packing case, blazed around it, making the junk piles glimmer like a sea-bottom of watery pewter.

Then, abruptly, the beam went out and the car drove away.

He hid all morning inside a dumpster in the alley, watching the lot from under the lid.

Everything was normal. At six-thirty the two passengers met at the bus stop and passed their package. The little girls invaded the field, playing baseball today. The imp climbed tirelessly up and down the fence. The dry-cleaner's wife visited the barbershop – 'Closed.'

At eleven o'clock the neighborhood gang attacked the lot for the first time in months. They doused the packing case with gasoline and set it on fire, then ran off, yelling and dancing. The straw and mattress and everything he owned burst into a volcano of flames.

A crowd gathered in the street and watched. The little girls lined the fence and cheered.

Inside the dumpster, Joe wondered where he would sleep tonight. Maybe he would just stay here, lounging in the rubbish until the next dumping. It was safe and cozy, and there were plenty of edibles. He laughed, letting his mind sink as far down as it could go. Maybe it would be easier, just to flip out, to loosen all the screws and surrender what was left of his wits to gibbering madness once and for all.

A bus pulled up to the stop. One passenger got off.

It was her.

He wasn't surprised. He'd been expecting her.

She walked into the lot and stood gazing at the fire.

He squirmed out from under the lid, jumped down into the alley and ran for his life.

11

He wobbled up Bell Street, all the way to Decatur, lurching and tottering like a cripple.

Then he stopped, lost. Which way now? Where was his car? Snow. He looked around, the bright sun warming his numbed muscles. Why wasn't it snowing? No … hold it! This wasn't Raleigh. He'd left there the night of the blizzard. He'd gone to … to … where? And he'd sold the BMW. In Atlanta. That's where he was now. What the fuck was he doing in Atlanta?

And who was *that?*

He gaped at a mirror in the window of a drugstore.

A ragged ghost stared back at him – hairy, bearded, wild-eyed, wrapped in a filthy blanket. He held up his hands. They were as sticky and grimy as crocodile claws. Jesus Christ! What had happened to him?

He walked on, limping, light-headed, stumbling, climbing slowly out of the abyss.

Lo the grass withers. And how! He was a wreck. Okay. She'd found him. But now she had to catch him. And in the meantime, he needed a cup of coffee. And he had to wash his hands … wow! How long had he been like this?

People passed, turning away from him, making faces. A little boy looked at him and laughed. His mom pulled him away, scolding him.

He asked a natty fellow in a three-piece suit for a dollar.

'Get a job, asshole!'

Another guy told him to go fuck himself. A pretty woman just snarled at him like a tiger.

He couldn't blame them. He was a nightmare. Freddy Kruger!

In Butler Park, he saw an elderly rabbi sitting on a bench. He limped over to him, trying not to look drunk.

'I don't want a drink,' he said. 'I just want to get cleaned up.'

'That would help,' the old guy grinned at him. 'You lost a shoe.'

Joe looked down. His left foot was scabby and black, covered with a ripped sock. 'It probably fell off when I jumped out of the dumpster. I can get a new pair for about two bucks. At the Goodwill Mart. Second hand. I need a razor too. And some clothes.'

'And soap.'

'Yeah right. Soap. It would only take …' he counted on his spotted fingers. 'Oh, all in all… about ten bucks.'

'And you want me to invest in you?'

'No, not really. Who gives away that kind of money? I'm just thinking out loud. A quarter would be fine.'

The rabbi gave him a cigar. And a fifty-dollar bill!

He bought everything at the Mart for less than fifteen bucks. Shoes, trousers, socks, a shirt, a sweater, a razor, a bar of soap.

He went into an alley behind the Federal Building and bathed at a spigot. He scrubbed his feet until they were raw. He hacked at his hair with a razor blade, then shaved off what was left, leaving his skull as nude as a stone. His beard too vanished, dropping away like wads of malignant seaweed. Then he dressed, feeling clean and sane for the first time since last winter. Was it last winter? Or the winter before that?

He went back to the park to show the rabbi the result. But he was gone.

He never smoked the cigar. He carried it in his pocket like a holy relic until it crumbled to nothingness.

12

At a snackbar, he ate a hamburger and drank three cups of coffee.

Then he made up his mind to try his luck again. Now or never! Not in East Point, no, the stakes there were too gigantic. There was an around-the-clock poker game in Deerwood Park. He had thirty dollars left. That was enough.

The card den was in an abandoned store on a back street. Three tables. Working class. He felt as conspicuous as a leper, but he must have looked okay, because nobody bothered him.

That's where he met Maxie Hearn. She was a cheerful redhead wearing big earrings. When he first saw her, she was standing in a corner, naked to the hips, sticking a Catapres-TTS patch between her breasts. Watching her inviting waist, he thought for just an instant about – he couldn't believe it – sex. But only faintly and briefly.

'High blood pressure,' she said. 'Catch it early and you live to be a hundred and ten.' She pulled on her blouse. 'Are you betting on the basketball game?'

'No. What are they playing here?'

'Just draw. Take the second table. It's warm. What happened to your hair? Are you a skinhead?'

'All the soldiers in my regiment shave their heads. Otherwise the Apaches would try to scalp us.'

'Oh, brother.'

As soon as there was an empty chair he sat down. He played for twelve hours. When he finally left, he had two thousand three hundred in his pocket. The hoodoo was broken!

He found Maxie in a bar across the street.

'I lost six big ones on the basketball game,' she groaned. 'I don't know why I even bother betting on sports. Basketball, baseball, football, volleyball. It must be hormonal. All those sweaty jocks just turn me on and I lose all sense of proportion. How did you do?'

'I got enough to buy a bus ticket.'

'I'm going to Nashville. You can come with me if you pay for the gas.'

Since he had to get away from here as soon as possible, he accepted. An hour later they were in her Toyota, speeding toward Chattanooga.

'Don't you have any stuff?' she asked.

'Stuff?'

'Like luggage.'

'I keep everything in my head.'

'Oh, brother!'

Driving through Damascus, he saw a billboard in a field. 'HO! HO! HO! JUST 60 MORE SHOPPING DAYS TILL XMAS!' As they passed, the 60 changed to 59.

That's when he composed his song.

Ho! ho! ho! ho!
Just go Joe go go go!
She'll get you if you go too slow!

'I try to take a week off from the cards every two or three months,' she said. 'Otherwise my blood pressure fluctuates like mad.'

She'd been playing poker and bridge ever since she left high school. She usually won enough every year to buy a condo. She owned apartments in St. Louis, Indianapolis, Louisville and KC. 'I'm looking into a couple of places in Nashville. You interested in investing?'

'Nope.'

'What do you do with your money?'

Couldn't she tell just by looking at his fingernails that he didn't do anything with it because he didn't have any. It made him feel better. Maybe he wasn't as visibly dilapidated as he thought.

'He started losing.' (Now she was talking about her ex-husband.) 'As soon as we were married he couldn't win anything. He said I put the hoodoo on him. Then I began to lose too. A double-hoodoo yet! Well, that relationship lasted about five minutes. I've got a house in Santa Monica.' (Back to real estate.) 'Just a small place. Properties are lousy there, because of the rent control. I think he's in New York now.' (Her husband again.) 'Living with a couple of guys. He's not a fag. I mean they're all probably straight, even if they are living together. Up and down! Up and down!' (Her blood pressure.) 'Sometimes a hoodoo can last a couple of years.' (Back to cards.) 'You ever gone through that?'

'Oh, yeah. For sure. Long endless hoodoos.'

'Not me. Knock on wood. These last eighteen months have been pretty peachy. But I can't keep it stabilized.' (Blood pressure.) 'That's why I wear a patch. Catapres-TTS. That means transdermal therapeutic systems. You just stick it on and forget about hypertension for a week. I change it every Saturday morning at nine a.m. Depending on what time zone I'm in. I'm thinking about buying an apartment in Las Vegas.' (Real estate.) 'A nifty place on Spring Mountain Road, not far from the Frontier Hotel. How did you lose your hair really?'

They stopped for the night in a motel in Tracy City. He spent an hour under the shower, scouring himself over and over again, scraping away every last trace of Atlanta.

Lieutenant, sir!

What is it, sergeant?

Atlanta is ours and fairly won!

Good. Burn it.

B-burn it, sir? Surely you …

You heard me. Put the city to the torch.

But, sir, what about Rhett Butler and Scarlet O'Hara?

'Hey, you!'

'Yes, Maxie?'

'Who're you talking to in there?'

'Nobody. Just myself. That's the only way I can get an intelligent answer.'

'Oh, brother!'

They slept together. But no matter how hard she tried, he couldn't rise to the occasion.

She didn't mind. They became good friends.

13

In Santa Monica, on the edge of Venice, was a Victorian mansion housing the 4 Straight Club, the Mecca of every poker player in the US. Its roster of members, past and present, was impressive: John Wayne, Alfred Hitchcock, Diane Keaton, John Ford, Richard Nixon, Liv Ullmann, Prince Andy, Fellini, Howard Hawks, Gore Vidal, etc.

Joe went directly there from the airport, only to learn that the membership fee was three thousand dollars.

He moved into a fleatrap on Wilshire Boulevard and during the next few days spent some of his meagre funds outfitting himself more presentably – including the purchase of an inevitable valise or two to allay management suspicion.

He went to the beach every day for an hour until the sun turned his shaven skull a bright pink.

He wasn't worried. The hoodoo was over. He had almost a grand. He just needed a few dollars more.

A bartender told him to look up a hooker named Ida, near the Santa Monica Pier. He found her and she introduced him to her pimp, who wanted twenty dollars for the information. Joe paid him and that same night knocked on a door on Ocean Park Boulevard. He was led down into a basement filled with panting men and women clutching fistfuls of money, crowded around a crap table.

He began by making side-bets. He lost a hundred, lost fifty more, lost another hundred. Then he began winning.

Two hundred, three, four, five. He lost half of that, won it back, lost it again, won again.

When he finally accepted the dice he threw three straight sevens. Six grand. By midnight he had his membership money, plus more than enough to pay his rent at the fleatrap for the next couple of months.

A man with a jack o'lantern face was watching him sullenly.

'You're doin okay, baldy,' he sneered. 'You brung your own dice with you?' He had a doghouse accent and was wearing a green suit, a yellow tie and a red shirt. He looked like a salad bar. 'Watch this hustler,' he yelled. 'Who is he anyhow? Anybody ever seen him before?'

'Ibn Kasim sent him,' somebody said.

'Ibn Kasim,' he smirked at Joe. 'What're you, a pimp too?'

Joe couldn't believe it. Who needed this shit? A run-in with a creep was to be avoided at all costs.

He left.

He was back at the 4 Straight bright and early the next morning. He paid his fee and was issued one of the club's famous membership cards – a grinning joker with an antic face, captioned, *'I Pass.'*

The doorman, a midget in a tux named Roscoe, led him into the games room. 'Show me your hands,' he ordered. According to club legend, he could spot a card-sharp instantly, just by looking at his fingers.

'You got the shakes, dude.' He examined Joe's knuckles and fingertips. 'You on speed or something?'

'I'm excited.'

'No need to be. Unless you're planning to rip us off. In which case you'll be deported to Bakersfield.' He scowled at the palm. 'What do we have here?'

'You read palms too?'

'I do. You got a funny life-line, pal, all crooked and zigzag.'

'Is that portentous?'

'P-o-r-t-e-n-t-o-u-s,' he spelled out the letters. 'I can spell any word you throw at me. I got an ear for syllables. Don't think just because I'm an insignificant little fellow that I'm an illiterate dork. Jerry Lewis once asked me how to spell *shalom aleichem* and I got it right on the first try.'

'Tell me about my life-line. No … on second thought, don't bother. Forget it.'

14

The room was an enormous rotunda with stained glass windows, filled with hundreds of tables. It was only eight o'clock but there were already scores of games in progress. Joe bought a thousand dollars worth of chips and waited for an invitation. That was one of the rules, never sit down without permission.

'Chair open!' someone called.

Dominating his stage fright, he sat down at a table with four blank-faced men who all gave him a fast once-over. They all saw the same thing. A bronzed youngster with a shaven head and a condescending smile. A smartass. They tagged him: 'Neophyte.' He'd probably last less than a week. They'd move in on him for a fast fleece before he threw in the towel and went back to Kansas or Idaho.

One of them wore a baseball cap, one a stetson, one a kepi. Obviously their good luck hats. The fourth was the same jack o'lantern-faced ballbreaker he'd encountered last night.

'Baldy!' he yodeled. 'They let pimps in here now?' To the others: 'This dude's got ten chicks out on the streets suckin cocks while he's sittin here lookin mean. What's the 4 Straight comin to I ask yous!'

Joe ignored him. So did the hats. Cards were all they were interested in, not bullshit.

Rattled, Joe folded on the first hand. Pumpkin-face was getting to him. That would never do. This was too important.

With an effort, he concentrated on his cards, oblivious of everything else – except that baleful shithead staring at him across the table. He folded again, losing more precious chips.

Roscoe the midget marched over to them. 'Ladies are complaining about the language you guys are using,' he warned. 'Knock it off.'

'We was just wonderin about the membership rules,' Jack O snickered. 'Aren't there regulations about keepin bums outta here?'

'You behave, Milch.'

'Not that I got any objections, as long as he minds his manners and just keeps foldin like Mr. Nice Schlep.'

Joe had to fold a third time. As soon as someone shouted 'Vacant chair!' he changed tables.

'Good riddance!' Milch yelped after him.

His new opponents were more congenial. A stunning Air France stewardess, an Army Colonel, a lady smoking Players and a Movie Star. Joe was immediately at ease. He won the first pot – and the second and third. This was more like it.

He continued to win more than he lost all morning and all afternoon. The stewardess flew off to Paris and was replaced by a man in a wheelchair. The Movie Star left and was replaced by a girl wearing gym togs and carrying a shopping bag filled with chips. The Players smoker left and was replaced by Milch.

'You still here, hairless?' he sniggered at Joe. 'Nobody caught you cheatin yet?'

Joe immediately got up and cashed in his chips. Eight grand. Way to go!

It was six-thirty. He had dinner at Bruno's in Venice then went back to his Wilshire fleatrap and slept like a log.

He was back in the rotunda the next day – and the next and the next. In five weeks he estimated that he'd spent about a thousand hours at the tables.

He now had his favorite adversaries. Wheelchair was one. He was a retired tycoon from La Jolla. Another was Mademoiselle Air France, when she was in town. The Movie Star was another. Joe often went to parties at his Bel Air estate and played tennis with him at the Brentwood Country Club.

There were others. A one-time senator who held the record for sitting in the longest stud game in California history – 72 hours nonstop. A sailor based in San Diego who spent all his winnings building a yacht. A screen-writer with four ex-wives and nine kids. An opera diva who showed up one night after a performance still wearing her *Aida* costume.

And, of course, there was Milch. Joe had programed himself to play with the loud-mouth shithead whenever he had a chance and thoroughly enjoyed out-bluffing him over and over again. He kept a careful account of the amounts won from him – so far ten grand. Half of it in IOUs.

Joe would have gladly given up poker for something else that paid as well. It was an exhausting way to make a living. It sapped your strength and turned the brain to quagmire. But where else could he earn a thousand dollars an hour?

But for all these other people – these fanatics and zealots – poker went far beyond winning or losing pots of chips. The game was their quest for the Holy Grail, obsessing them in a lifelong captivation more consumptive than love or religion or crack. They were explorers trudging one behind the other in a safari through the jungles and deserts of a million games, searching for the lost city of Ophir, in the Valley of Delight, and every deal was another step toward the discovery of their heart's desire.

He couldn't understand their passionate dedication. He always knew what cards they were hiding. Milch's maniac eyes would burn with frenzy over a pair. Miss Air France would go into orgasmic spasms with three of a kind. The Movie Star would sit petrified with helpless ecstasy when he was dealt the queen that would build his full house.

Even Wheelchair, the fabled corporation czar, the Attila of the boardroom, would blush like a maiden, speechless and agog over a good hand.

Joe's own cool lack of fervor made him realize that he was at long last becoming a pro.

And he felt that he was missing something.

15

He opened an account at the California Overseas Bank in Marina del Rey. His hair grew. He read hundreds of books. He began smoking cigars.

There was one dreary hoodoo period when he lost almost everything but within two months he won it all back again.

He was still living in his Wilshire fleatrap and was looking around for a new place. But apartments in Santa Monica were hard to find and in LA they were outrageously over-priced. He didn't want to invest in anything expensive and permanent. He was afraid that being too comfortably installed would make him lazy and careless. He had to be able to bolt at a moment's notice.

Then one morning while he was talking to Roscoe in the foyer, an old acquaintance strolled into the 4 Straight. A redhead, wearing earrings as heavy as golfballs.

'Here's one for you, shorty,' she said. *'Vaginismus.'*

'Easy!' the midget beamed. 'V-a-g-i-n-uhh-i-s-m-u-s.'

'Correct. And I hope it never happens to you. Hi, Joe.'

'Hi, Maxie.'

They had breakfast together at Bob's on Ocean Park. She'd just flown in from a bridge tournament in Mexico City. Since she'd last seen him she'd sold her condo in KC and bought two more in Colorado Springs and Cedar Rapids. She'd also visited her husband in New York. 'He's pumping iron now and living with a bus driver in the Bronx. Talk about out-of-the-closet! Brother! He's so gay he's merry. A muscle-bound hulk wearing fake eyelashes. I haven't even been to my Santa Monica joint yet. I hope it's still there. I mean, all these earthquakes. I was with a guy the night before last who was so huge he couldn't get it in. I swear, his cock was bigger than a dinosaur's tail. Do you still have a problem?'

'What problem?'

'Come on, Joe. Confide in Sister Maxie.'

'Oh, you mean getting it up? I don't think about things like that.'

'So what do you do instead of things like that?'

'I meditate.'

'Oh, brother. I met a friend of yours in Des Moines. Last March.'

'I don't know anybody in Des Moines. Where the hell is it anyway? Utah?'

'Iowa. A nifty chic-looking blonde with long legs and big eyes.'

His stomach contracted. 'Maxie, I think that might be someone ...' His coffee suddenly tasted like ink. 'Someone I'd like to avoid seeing. How did you meet her?'

'I was walking along Fleur Drive on my way to a

realtor's office and she was standing in front of the Bible College. "You're Maxie," she said. Just like that. "Yeah," I said. "Who are you?" And she said, "I'm a friend of Joe Egan's. Do you by any chance know where I can get in touch with him?"'

'What did you tell her?'

'Nothing. I didn't know where you were.'

'Good.'

'She was really a knock-out. Like a cover of *Vogue.*'

'Did she say anything else?'

'Yeah. She asked me why you shaved off your hair.'

They went to her house on Eleventh Street. A small place, only half-furnished, but clean and tidy. She invited him to move in with her for three hundred a month. He jumped at the chance. It was an ideal hideout, only twenty minutes to the airport and just a few blocks from the Santa Monica Freeway. He'd have to buy a car.

They lived together for a year, sleeping in separate beds, spending most of their time at the club. They'd leave in the morning and come home at night, like colleagues working in the same office. Milch snarled and called them 'Mr. and Mrs. Schmuck.'

'Don't pay any attention to Milch,' she told him. 'He's got a problem. He's been busted twice for transvestism. Can you imagine that repulsive hyena in drag? It's beyond belief! He made a deal with the cops the last time they collared him. They use him as a decoy. He swishes around Hollywood Boulevard in an evening gown, picking up guys who're into kink, then turns them over to the Vice Squad.'

She dragged Joe all over LA and Orange Counties, inspecting properties. They went to several of the Movie Star's parties and spent some weekends at Wheelchair's palace in La Jolla. Since her unfortunate sexual encounter in Mexico City, she'd sworn off men for a while and had a brief affair with Miss Air France.

And, except for the debits and credits of the poker games, life was smooth and pleasant.

And yet …

Any sign of the Apaches, Sergeant?

No, sir, Lieutenant. It's mighty quiet out there.

Yes indeed. Too *quiet.*

He couldn't forget Des Moines. How had she known about Maxie? And how did she find out he'd shaven his head? She must have been making inquiries all the way from the poker den in Deerwod Park to Nashville. Like a detective. Tracking him down, looking for his footprints. She probably even had a photo of him.

Do you know this man?

Yeh, I think so. Looks like the guy who was in here yesterday playin cards. No hair. Bald as a cueball. He left with Maxie Hearn in her Toyota. They went to Nashville. What're you after him for, lady?

I want to kill him.

How could he lose her? A foolish question! Or was it? He'd done it before, he could do it again. And again and again. But he had to have some kind of a head start on her. A … what did they call it? A coign of vantage. Maybe he should go to Mass again. Or change his name. Or disguise himself …

Now he was just being silly.

16

His skill at cards brought about his downfall.

Coming back to the club after lunch one day in April, he was astonished to find all the tables empty. Not a single game was in progress. All the players were on their feet, cheering and applauding.

Roscoe banged a staff on the floor and blared, 'Make way! Make way!'

The ex-senator made a speech. Caterers served champagne. Joe was presented with a new 'Royal Golden' membership card and a check for $10,000. Then he was ceremoniously escorted to a throne in the center of the rotunda.

And he was coronated.

The event was written up in the second page of the *Herald Examiner.* There was a photo of Joe, enthroned, wearing his crown and holding a scepter, under the headline: '4 *STRAIGHT CLUB CROWNS POKER KING OF THE YEAR.*'

He was appalled.

His name, his address, his picture ... yike! She'd come after him now faster than lightning.

How much time did he have?

A car! Shit! He should have a car. He'd kept putting off buying one, now it was too late.

He went to his bank and withdrew everything, closing his account. No … he didn't need a car. He didn't want to find himself stranded on some lonely country road out of gas or with a flat tire.

He took a cab back to the house. He tried to pack, not knowing what to take. Suit, some shirts, ties, a raincoat, an overcoat. He was in the middle of reading *The Brothers Karamazov,* he'd have to take that too. He had a whole god-damned library of unread books. *Cities of the Plain, Napoleon, From Reverence to Rape, A Stillness at Appomattox, The Red Knight of Germany* … fuck it! He wouldn't take anything. Just a few cigars.

Besides, he was being asinine. This was over-reacting to the point of idiocy. How many newspapers were there in America? She couldn't read them all. One column on page 2 of the *Examiner* was about as noticeable as Uranus.

He took a hot bath to soothe his jangling nerves. King of the Year! Christ! How could he have let that happen? He was like one of those yokels in ancient Greece, chosen during the germinal season to be an imitation monarch, then, at harvest time, sacrificed to Dionysus or somebody – torn to pieces limb by limb, butchered, mangled … Jesus! He was right smack back at the lake, in the Temple of Cadenza.

He'd never grown up, that was his trouble. He played cards with some mature intelligence, but in everything else he was juvenile. Adults faced their problems rationally … sensibly … *sanely* … A child was always on the borderline of lunacy, oblivious of logic.

Okay. He'd be logical. What was it Father Patrick had told him? *If she really wanted to find you, she couldn't be fooled.* Right. All she had to do was punch the right keys on the Master Computer and there he was. *EGAN Joseph.* Why hadn't she done that? But she had! She'd traced him to Atlanta through his credit cards. Hadn't she? And she could just as easily find him in LA through his bank account at California Overseas. And she hadn't. So what difference did the *Examiner* story make? Was she or wasn't she infallible? That was the question. After all, a colossal organization like the FBI wasn't flawless. They searched for fugitives for years and years in vain. Maybe she was capable of blundering too.

He shaved, dressed.

So? To run or not to run? One thing was certain, he wouldn't go back to the club. No way. So there was really no reason to stay in LA.

It was ten o'clock. The mail came at ten-thirty. He'd wait that long to make up his mind.

He tried to read a chapter of *The Brothers K.* The words scattered across the page like ants.

Her meeting Maxie in Des Moines didn't mean anything. That could have been simply an accident. Yeah sure. Like the iceberg hitting the *Titanic.* What the hell was a Master Computer?

He glanced out the window.

She was standing on the pavement, talking to the mailman.

17

He crossed the back yard, climbed over the fence, jumped into the alley.

There was no panic this time. He felt strangely jubilant. He'd out-guessed her again. He was free and on the move.

He hurried down Ashland to Lincoln Boulevard.

He'd had his rest, he'd won some money. Now it was *go go go!* He'd miss Maxie. Would she report his disappearance to the police? Missing persons? No … that wasn't her style. She was just as migrant as he was. Unexpected arrivals and sudden departures were normal.

He bought a postcard and a stamp at a Thrifty Store and scribbled a goodbye.

> *Had to take off. Say so long for me at the club. I'll let you know where I am. J.*

He mailed it, then caught a bus to LAX. Then he changed his mind about flying out. The airport would be the first place she'd check. No? Suppose she was waiting for him on the plane? God!

He took a cab downtown and bought a bus ticket to Fresno.

He spent the night there, then flew to Salt Lake City, spent three nights there, then flew to New Orleans, spent a week there, then flew to St. Petersburg, Florida. At Clearwater Airport he felt immediately at home. It was windy and raining, Tampa Bay was thrashing like a boiling cauldron, the sky was leaden. But the vibes were harmonious and the air was clean. His restlessness faded.

He'd picked up a valise and some clothes in Fresno, so he was presentable enough. He checked into a motel on Fourth Street.

He bought a money-belt for his cash and his 'Royal Golden' card, then put everything in a safe-deposit box in a bank around the corner.

He did absolutely nothing for a month, except walk the streets, wandering about Pinelass Park and Treasure Island.

He didn't even buy any books. He cut down on his smoking. Three cigars a day.

He found a town called Safety Harbor and was on the point of moving there – because of its inviting name – when, one morning, he saw in the paper that a Nellie Jarman was having an exhibit in an art gallery in Tampa.

The name meant something to him. Jarman … Jarman … Nellie … an echo from long ago and far away.

Sure! The Dean's daughter at Dad's university!

Secrets. Professor Benton, the history teacher, was gay. Owlish Madam Manners, the General's widow, snorted coke. Peggy-Sue Morgan and Dr. Robert's nurse were lovers. Et cetera. And Nellie was a congenital shoplifter.

And yeah! Hey! Hadn't they made it together? He couldn't recall. Though he did remember that he'd taught her how to play poker.

He took a taxi to Tampa. The gallery was on Hillsborough Avenue, a big glass rectangle crowded with assholes. The pictures on display looked like gaudy tick-tack-toe games. All were boldly signed *'NEL.'*

He found her sitting in a circle of fawning admirers, wrapped in a red sari, wearing jogging shoes, eating an ice-cream cone.

She was absolutely gorgeous! He winked at her, beckoned. She drifted over to him, her lovely cat's eyes narrowing.

'Greetings, Nellie.'

'Let me see …' she had a lazy drawl now, very Deep South and caressing. 'Your daddy was in the math department.'

'Music.'

'You had a canoe.'

'Right.'

'Your favorite movie star was Catherine Deneuve.'

'And yours was Orson Welles. I met him in Los Angeles. He's a friend of a friend of mine.'

'I invited you up to my room to listen to my Shakespeare records and you raped me.'

'No I didn't.'

'Or I raped you.'

'That must have been somebody else.'

'I'll have to consult my diary. What do you think of my paintings! Stop! I'm sorry I asked. Your expression of obtuse nausea indicates terminal Philistinism, so just never mind.'

'I hate that word.'

'Philistinism?'

'Terminal.'

They had lunch in an Italian cellar in Temple Terrace. He really didn't have anything to say to her, but she enjoyed discussing herself and he just let her ramble.

'I married Speed Evans. You remember him.'

'Speed Evans! Certainly!' He remembered especially Professor Benton gobbling him on the Isle.

'It lasted about a year.' (Longer than Roxie's marriage – five minutes!) 'Then he went out west to coach some rustic football team. And I went to Berlin. And Florence. And other places. I sold my first painting to the Duchess of Proel. Do you know who she is?'

'Nope.'

'You must have heard of her, Egan, she's famous.'

'I've heard of the Duchess of Malfi.'

'She's on talkshows all the time. I met her in Capri. She was lying on the beach, sunbathing, utterly *à poil!* I painted her portrait. What a heavenly creature! We had a liaison naturally. It was grand. There's something about cunnilingus with a duchess that's highly arousing. The climaxes are intensely snobbish. One must suppose it's class related. After going down on me, she'd say things like, "Precious Nellie, you mustn't shave your legs. Hairy little girls are *le dernier cri* this season."' She picked up an ashtray and a spoon, slipped them into her handbag. 'Anyway, I settled here four years ago. I bought a loft. Do you want to go there and – pray excuse the circumlocution – fuck?'

'I guess not, Nel.'

'I've often wondered whatever became of you.'

He didn't believe that. But it was lulling, listening to her drawl. She was feline and melodious and smelled of lilacs. She suspended him in languor. He wished he could doze off and find her still there when he woke. Was this all he had to look forward to, just this? Brief moments of peace in the eye of the storm?

He steered her back into the past. 'Nellie, do you remember Morgan?'

'Vaguely. Oh, yes. Morgan. Horses, the riding academy. He lived on Greenwood Avenue.'

'Right.'

'We tried to buy his house. Speed and I. But it was all tied up in an inheritance squabble.'

'Do you remember how he died?'

'He toppled out of the saddle while under the influence, as I recall.'

'Yes.'

'Why do you ask?'

'Oh, just seeing you brings it all back … the lake, the canoe, Shakespeare, Greenwood Avenue, people, nostalgia. "The past is a foreign country, they do things differently there." Who said that?'

'Why don't you want to screw me?'

'I'm a uhh Catholic.'

'Did you ever get married?'

'Yes.'

'Anyone I know?'

'No. A girl from Oklahoma City. I met her in Raleigh.'

'It's a small world. That's where Speed is teaching. Oklahoma.' She frowned. 'His niece went mad.'

'Speed's niece?'

'Morgan's niece. What was her name?'

'Peggy-Sue.'

'They locked her up in the looney bin.'

'How did that happen?'

'She began wandering around town like a banshee, telling everybody she actually saw The Angel of Death.'

18

He flew home the next day. He didn't go to the lake. The asylum was in Cooperstown. If Peggy-Sue were still alive, that's where she'd be.

The place was called Wildflower Downs and he had no trouble at all getting past the girl at the reception desk. She clipped a tag on his lapel and told him Peg was out in the garden.

It wasn't a garden. It was a courtyard with a few trees and hedges. It reminded him of his vacant lot in Atlanta. A dozen lost souls in tan smocks were sitting in the afternoon sunshine, watching two nurses pitch horseshoes. He asked an old fellow reading a comic book where Peggy-Sue was.

'Sue due few,' the man muttered. 'Two you blue new dew pew one-two.'

Another patient, darning a sock, pointed to a woman sitting at the far end of the enclosure. 'That's Peggy,' he said. 'Are you her lawyer?'

'No, just a friend.'

'Nobody has any friends in here,' he grunted. 'We're on our own.'

'Own,' the first man recited. 'Home bone stone

poem comb loan dome roam …'

Peggy-Sue was sitting on a bench, eating a prune. He was surprised how young she looked, then realized she was only about five or ten years older than he was. She was gray haired, black eyed and, like Maxie, was wearing weighty earrings.

'Another attorney,' she sighed. 'About the house, I suppose. Well, I still own it and I'm not going to let anyone take it away from me.'

'No, Peg. I'm Joe Egan.'

'That house belongs to me. It's mine. Shithead left it to me in his will. So don't try to drop me into some loophole.'

'Joe Egan.'

'I know who you are. No need to keep repeating it over and over again. I sang in your papa's choir for two years. You used to walk past the house every morning going to school.'

'Yes.'

'Come along with me,' she got up, took him by the arm, led him behind a wall. 'Nobody can see us here. Not that it matters. Nobody in this pigsty gives a shit about anything. Walter, the head orderly, is the only decent human being here. He likes to rub his cock on my tits. That's a lot of fun.' She kissed him on the cheek, licked his ear. Her hands slid to his belt, fumbled with it.

Startled, he looked around. But she was right. No one could see them. A squirrel hopped out of a tree, picked up what was left of her prune.

'Tell me about the Angel of Death, Peggy-Sue.'

'She rang the doorbell,' Peg said. 'I was in the

kitchen, doing the dishes. Uncle Shithead was watching TV. "Who's that?" he yelled. "Peg, go see who's there!" I looked out the window. That's when I saw her. Standing on the porch. Nobody believes me.'

'I believe you.'

'I bet.'

'I do.'

His belt was unbuckled. She dropped to her knees, pulled down his trousers. She nibbled on his thigh, squeezed him. He didn't try to stop her.

'"It's the Angel of Death," I told him. "She's come to get you, shithead!" "I'll disinherit you, you little bitch," he says. "You won't have time to," I says.'

'What did she look like, Peg?'

'Like a nun. With a hood on. All in black. Carrying a scythe on her shoulder.'

'A scythe?'

He was in her mouth now, her tongue lapping him hungrily. Then she leaned back, looked up at him. 'I opened the front door and she came into the living room.'

'Then what happened?'

'He screamed. What's the matter, can't I get it hard? Not that I'm complaining mind you. A cock is a cock, few and far between.'

'What happened then?'

'I ran out to the street.' Her lips took him tightly. He felt a feeble stirring – just a spark. Yes! No … There it was again. An electric tingling. She stopped. 'I went to the drugstore and had a strawberry shake. When I came back he was deceased. That's what Dr. Roberts said, "Deceased." She wasn't there, the blond Angel. I never told nobody. They'd think I was a fruitcake.' She laughed. 'It's my fault. I've been in this dungeon so long I forget how to turn a guy on.'

She sat down on the ground and watched the squirrel.

'A scythe ...?' he pulled up his trousers, buttoned them quickly. 'She was carrying a scythe?'

'You think I'm lying. You think I *belong* here.'

'No. I saw her too.'

'Everybody tells me that. Just to humor me.'

'But she didn't have a scythe. She looked ... I don't know. Just as normal as anyone else.'

'You're putting me on! You saw her?'

'Yes.'

'He's one of us!' she called across the yard. 'Sign him in! Always room for one more!' She jumped up. 'But I saw her again.'

'Where did you see her?'

'On Grant Street, standing by the bookstore. That's when I started telling everybody. To warn them. And they put me in here.'

'Did you talk to her?'

'I almost didn't, I was so scared. She looked *mean.* Then I asked her if she came back for me this time. She didn't have her scythe. She was wearing a black dress. She was very very furious. I could see that. Even though she was smiling. But she didn't want me. She was looking for somebody else. Do you want to try again? I'm not wearing anything under my smock. It seems like a shame, not squirting you off.'

'Who, Peggy-Sue? Who was she looking for?'

'For you.'

19

He flew back to St. Petersburg the next morning. He had a fever, his eyes were burning, his ears ringing. At the motel, he swallowed three Tylenol gelcaps and tried to sleep.

A scythe! Wow!

He believed her though. There was no doubt in his mind that she was telling the truth. Oh, no. It was the old eye-of-the-beholder principle. People just *see* what they *see*. And the beheld can take any form the eye devises. Walking along Greenwood Avenue, a little boy saw a blonde in a black coat. And five minutes later, looking out the window, Peggy-Sue saw a medieval shape of Death, holding a scythe.

What would the Board of Shrinks have to say about that?

Obviously collective fantasizing. And, I might add, typical in cases of duo-hallucinatory sexual ambiguity. And, of course, it goes without saying, a repressed pas de deux*-like transference of voyeuristic and guilty penis-envy – the scythe in question being the perfect allegorical phallus, with a cutting edge that when turned upside-down resembles an erection …*

The phone rang.

His temperature climbed even higher as he lay there listening to it. Finally, he picked up the receiver. 'Room service,' he rasped.

'Egan?'

It was only Nellie, inviting him to dinner. When he told her he was ill she came rushing across the bay with a doctor, a young woman named Alice. She gave him an injection of something and he immediately felt much better.

'Alice is a surgeon,' Nel explained. 'She adores cutting up patients and extracting their innards. Especially males.'

'Males have no innards,' Alice said. 'They're all hollow façades.'

The three of them went to a seafood place in Palm Harbor. The two girls talked about Nellie's exhibit. She'd already sold twelve paintings for over five thousand each.

'Not bad,' Alice said. 'But he'll take it away from you. He's back, y'know.'

'No!'

'He got in yesterday.'

'The little prick! We'll nail him this time!'

Joe ate in silence. His sole meunière tasted like rubber.

'Egan,' Nellie took him by the hand. 'You taught me how to play, didn't you?'

Her touch was like balm. The sole was suddenly delicious. 'Mmm? Play? What? The violin?'

'We used to hide in a boathouse on the lake,' she turned to Alice, 'and play and neck all day long.'

'Neck?' Alice grimaced. 'That sounds like something ostriches do.'

'Didn't we, Egan?'

'Excuse me, Nel, but you've lost me.'

'Poker.'

'Oh, sure. Poker. My father taught me the game. And I taught you. Right.'

'There's a sonofabitch who shows up in Tampa periodically and cleans us out. We think he's cheating.'

'That's easy enough to spot.'

'I happen to be an excellent poker player,' Alice huffed, 'and I haven't been able to "spot" it.'

'He's very clever,' Nellie said.

'If he plays poker and has to cheat to win, then he isn't clever. Alice, for instance, is clever.' (Flatter the unfriendly slut.) 'If she couldn't win cleverly, she wouldn't play.'

'Poker is a simpleton's game,' she snapped down on a piece of lobster, like a parrot. 'And you don't know whether I'm clever or not, do you?'

'You have a high forehead.'

'Why don't you buy one of Nellie's paintings?'

Ah hah! She was wondering about his finances. His trousers and shirt and jacket were properly expensive, but just a bit too *new.* What did he *do?* How much was he *worth?*

'I can't afford it,' he sighed. Fuck her. Let her pick up the tab. She's the one who invited him to this clipjoint. 'I'm just a penniless architect.'

'Is that what you are?' Nel drawled. 'I forgot to ask. I …'

'What have you built?' Alice cut in.

'Just one small house,' he said. 'In Atlanta.'

20

The session took place the following evening, in Nellie's studio on Bayshore Road, a loft as large as three tennis courts, filled with canvasses and antiques and marijuana growing in casks.

She still loved Shakespeare. She had all his plays on cassettes. While Alice was making a phone call, they listened to Orson Welles in *Julius Caesar.*

'"*For our elders say,*"' she recited along with Edgar Battler's whispering voice, '"*the barren, touched in this holy chase, shake off their sterile curse.*" Egan, do you have any children?'

'Nope.'

'Me neither. Alas. I'd give anything to be pregnant.' She studied him. 'For that I need a stud.'

Alice switched off the machine and sat down beside her. 'Shakespeare was a fag,' she said. 'All those boys, dressed as girls. And vice versa. His ambivalence was pitiful.'

Joe was relieved. He'd been dreading having to listen to Act 2, Scene 2. '*X, a necessary end, will come when it will come,*' Christ! X! He couldn't even bring himself to pronounce the word now. He was really freaked out.

'Alice turns me on fiercely,' Nel drawled. 'But sperm has its charm.'

'Perhaps you can talk Egan into tearing off a quick one with you,' Alice stroked her hair.

'I already tried. He doesn't seem interested.'

'You probably intimidate him. Girls eager to bestow their favors on any dude available can be terribly threatening.'

'Or maybe he's – *oserais-je le dire?* – fruity?'

'Or just neuter. A blank cartridge.'

Joe smiled, settling deeper into sudden contentment, listening to them drone. This was another one of those odd moments of quiescence, when the vibes were appeasing. His wounds healed, all his loss and pain became soft music playing in a void. Where was Ada now? What was she doing? Children? No, they'd never have their baby before she was thirty. They'd never grow old together and watch the acorns turn to forests. The concerto would have no second or third movements. Their themes would just dissolve in empty oblivion.

'I think he's falling asleep,' Nellie said. 'All fagged out. He was always bizarre. He used to memorize requiems and do-it-yourself manuals. There was a horrible island in the lake, our parents wouldn't let us go anywhere near it, because of the watersnakes. But he was over there all the time, doing mysterious whimsical things.'

'Probably playing with himself,' Alice concluded.

Their guests arrived at eight. A hideous woman in a mauve dress and an orange coat, wearing a floppy hat.

It was Milch.

'You!' a snarl. 'Shit!'

'Mrs. Milch,' he waved. 'Hi. What a surprise.'

'What are you doing in Florida, asshole?'

'None of your business.'

'Fuck you!'

'Stop making faces, you'll demolish your pretty make-up. God! You look like Queen Victoria.'

'Don't mock me, you bastard!'

'You know each other?' Nellie asked. 'I find that highly *coup de theâtre*-ish.'

'They make a darling couple,' Alice remarked. 'Albeit chilling.'

'Always mockery!' Milch railed. 'Don't you think I know I'm ridiculous?'

'No you're not, Milch.' Nellie pinched his cheek. 'You're just dubious. Let's gamble.'

They played for five hours. Joe took six thousand from Milch, eight thousand from Nel and thirteen thousand from Alice.

At two o'clock in the morning he began to feel dizzy and knew immediately that the girls had put something in the coffee he'd been drinking.

He tried to get up and fell out of his chair.

21

'Joe!'

It was Ada, calling to him. In a parking lot. No, in a railroad station or an airport. Or on a roof. In a blizzard.

He woke.

He was lying on a bed, his arms spread, his wrists tied to the posts.

Alice was bending over him. 'He admitted everything,' she said. 'You were in it together, the two of you. You were going to rip us off then split the winnings.'

'That's a lie.'

'He told me you were kicked out of the 4 Straight Club in LA because you were caught cheating.'

'He's lying, Alice.'

Nellie came into the room. 'Oh, Egan,' she drawled. 'I'm so disappointed in you. You turned out to be a grubby little cardshark. How awful.' She leaned down and kissed him on the lips. It was almost agreeable.

'Untie me, Nellie. This is goofy.'

'No no no. You took advantage of our friendship to try to pick my pocket. I can never forgive you for that. And you're not an architect even!'

'Don't believe anything Milch tells you. He's a slob.'

'Y'know what we're going to do?' Alice grinned. 'We're going to tie you up and dump you in the street in front of the police station, dressed just as you are. Tampa cops know how to deal with drag queens.'

He looked down. He was wearing Milch's mauve dress! And the wig!

They turned out the lights and left him there in the dark.

In the studio, someone was playing a flute. Then three girls were singing and laughing. It sounded like a party.

God damn it! No cops. If he were booked on a morals charge that would be the end of everything. Even trying to talk his way out of it would be messy. If he was lucky they'd just rough him up and let him go. But if they hauled him in front of a judge he'd do time for sure. Florida laws were lethal.

He pulled and jerked his arms, freeing one wrist.

Then she looked through the window.

He saw her shadow first, lowering in the moonlight on the wall just beside him. He turned.

She was out on the balcony, staring into the room. She opened the window and came over to the bed. His heart stopped beating. He could hear it, thumping in his chest. Then – nothing! It *stopped.*

She peered down at him.

Then she went back out to the balcony.

His heart began drumming again. Blood flowed into his aching brain.

The wig! And the dress! She hadn't recognized him!

He was alive!

He yanked at the rope, pulling out the other wrist. Where was she?

He got up, his head spinning. Where did she go? He opened the door, went out into a hallway.

The loft was dim, filled with undressed girls. Nellie was dancing with an Amazon, both wrapped in a sheet, their lips fastened together. Two others were coiling around Alice, on the floor, like a spider with six weaving legs. Another was sitting on Milch's lap, blowing a flute. He was tied to a chair, gagged, his bulging eyes glaring at Joe.

Where was she?

He moved through the thickets of marijuana, went into the kitchen. He was walking on high heels, his heavy skirt pinioning his legs. He pulled off the shoes, unbolted the service door, stumped down a steep flight of steps to a parking lot.

He vomited in the gutter, emptying himself of pints of swill.

Just across Bayside was the beach. He saw a row of cabanas there. They meant clothes – maybe.

He crossed the road, ran through the sand. They were all unlocked. In the second one he found what he needed. He tore off the dress and wig, pulled on a pair of shorts and a ragged T-shirt.

She almost found him.

She was on the beach, coming straight toward him, as if he were her loadstone.

He picked up the dress and wig, climbed up to the cabana's slanting roof, stretched out on it, watched her.

She was wearing a black sheath, her blond hair tied

in a black band. In the moonlight, with the surf and the sand all around her, she looked glimmering and transparent.

'Joe!'

Oh, Jesus! She'd seen him.

No … not yet …

She opened the door of the first cabana, then the next and the next …

He hid his face in the dress.

She opened all the doors, one after the other. *His* door banged, just beneath his ear, jarring him. He uncovered one eye.

She was walking off. Up the beach to Bayside, into the street lights. Her hips were swaying.

He jumped off the roof and ran.

22

A truckdriver gave him a ride to Riverview. Then he walked south on 301. The sun came up, rising in thick stormy globs out of the middle of Florida. He was looking for a quiet wood where he could take a long nap under the trees.

Instead he found Iraq.

A Triumph was jacked up on the edge of a field, a tall black girl was changing the tire.

She spun around as he approached.

'It's all right,' he tried to smile, but his jaws were like pigiron. 'I'm not a highwayman.'

'Then just keep walking,' she said.

'Right.'

A car passed. He jumped behind the Triumph, dropped to his knees.

A huge bird flew over them, its wings flapping loudly.

'Look!' she cried. 'That's an albatross!'

'"*Instead of a cross an albatross about my neck was hung.*"' He tried to get up. His knees buckled. 'I memorized "The Rhyme of the Ancient Mariner" when I was a kid.'

'It's an auspicious sign.' She watched it fly off into

the amber overcast. 'So you're probably not as foreboding as you look.'

'In that case, I need a lift.'

'Fix my flat and I'll take you into Palmetto.'

'It's a deal.' He came around the car, reeling, almost falling. 'Excuse me, I'm lightheaded.'

'Me,' she grinned, 'I'm darkheaded.'

She was doing seventy. He wished she'd stop gazing at him and watch the road instead.

'My name is Joe.'

'Mine's Iraq Weber.'

She took a pendant on a chain from her pocket, hung it on the rearview mirror. He examined it. It was a silver cat with diamond eyes.

'What's this?'

'It will put you to sleep.'

'You're going too fast.'

'Aren't you in a hurry?'

'Yes, as a matter of fact. The faster the better.'

'What are you running from, Joe?'

'A card game. That reminds me … Nellie and Alice owe me … how much? Twenty grand? As for Milch, that mangy little weasel … I still have his IOUs in my moneybelt …' The diamonds glittered. 'In my safe-deposit box in … in … I never finished *The Brothers K* … you shouldn't pick up strangers on the road … for all you know I might be an ax-murderer …'

'Me too.'

'Your cat is looking at me evilly.'

'Not evilly, no.'

'Diamond eyes.'

'Where are your clothes?'

'Gone. Everything. All gone. Run run run …'

He sank into an ocean of peace.

He woke just in time to see a roadsign pointing to Palmetto in the opposite direction.

'Aren't we going to Palmetto?'

'No.'

'Where are we going … uh … what's your name again?'

'Iraq.'

'Where are you taking me, Iraq?'

'Farther on.'

He slept again.

23

He was still in the Triumph when he woke. It was parked in the carport of a house on the seaside. At first he thought he was back in his wooden box in the lot in Atlanta and that the sound of the waves was the traffic on Memorial Drive. But that was a long long time ago and this was Florida. And he was broke again, in a torn T-shirt and shorts, barefoot. Hoodoo.

He walked across a terrace high above the beach and went into the house through an open window. Into a sunny room with gray and yellow walls.

Iraq came out of the kitchen, wearing a bikini, peeling an orange.

'Come in,' she said.

'Where are we?'

'Naples. This is where I live. You'll be safe here. It's been immunized.'

'Immunized?' he stared at her legs. 'Against what?'

'This and that. What are you looking at?'

She was incredibly sensual, like a resplendent carnal feast. The slightest false note would have spoiled everything – a roll of the hips, a lascivious look, a boudoir smile – but she was grave and still, without falsehood. Only her eyes simmered and flashed.

'Would you care for a drink?'

'No thanks. Do you by any chance have some cigars on the premises?'

She had. A humidor filled with havanas. He lit one and it tasted divine.

'Iraq ...'

'Yes, Joe?'

'I think you have the wrong guy.'

'What does that mean?'

'I'm not good for anything. I'm a wreck. I can play poker, that's all. Everything else is decrepit. I should be wearing a sign: *"Malfunction."* I'm going on the road for a while, then I'm going to sneak back into Petersburg to my safe-deposit box. If you could loan me a little money, just enough to keep me going, I'll repay you before the end of the month.'

'In there,' she pointed. 'Take a bath and shave and put on some clothes.'

The bathroom was blue – tiles, ceiling, tub. Even the soap. On the windowsill violets grew in an azure pot. She was a young woman who chose everything carefully, with a sense of hues and rhymes. But why had she chosen *him?*

He looked at himself in the mirror. Not too grisly. He needed a haircut, but aside from that he was just as blankly nondescript as any normal person. Certainly not a morsel for this splendid black goddess.

He bathed and scrubbed his head with indigo shampoo.

On the bed in the guest room was a shopping bag. He unpacked gray corduroy trousers, a pair of sandals, a shirt, a leather sweater. He didn't check the sizes. He knew they would fit. What did she want?

He smoked another cigar.

They had dinner in a Spanish restaurant in East Naples. The Mexican maître d'hôtel oozed with reverence when they entered. The waiters were all Cuban and bowed respectfully like a chorus line.

'Are you the Mayor?' he asked. 'Or with Immigration or something?'

'They're afraid of me,' she whispered. 'Because of this.' She was wearing her cat pendant. She touched it with the tip of her finger. 'My charm.'

'They're afraid you might put them to sleep?'

'Worse,' she laughed. 'One evening the former maître d'hôtel was rude to me. A few moments later he scalded his hand on a stove in the kitchen. Another time, the bartender refused to serve me at the bar because I didn't have an escort. He even suggested I go across the street to a cafe where hookers hang out. The same night he was hit by a car in the parking lot. Do you really think I brought you to my house to sleep with me?'

'Sort of.'

'I didn't. I doubt very much if you're capable of sexual intercourse.'

Why did that embarrass him? It never had before. He felt suddenly ashamed, as if his inadequacy were important.

During the meal she told him a little about herself. Her parents were South African, members of the Batloka tribe, the Wild Cat People. Twenty years ago, a Dutch captain had smuggled them aboard his freighter and taken them to New Orleans, where they'd entered the United States illegally. Iraq was born in Mobile. She'd graduated from Alabama State and had worked in San Francisco, Chicago and New York. She was semi-retired now.

'Retired from what?'

'Guess.'

'You were a model.'

'True. For a while, when I was in my teens. I was even on the cover of *Elle.* Twice, in fact. But that's not it.'

'A Gospel singer? A tapdancer? A lion tamer?'

'No.'

'I give up.'

'I'm a medium.'

24

He slept in the guest room, without dreams or tension. He woke once in the middle of the night and thought he saw her kneeling on the floor beside the bed, holding a stick, tapping it silently on the rug. He tried to ask her what she was doing, but then the sun was shining and he was alone in the room.

They had breakfast on the terrace, then took a walk on the beach. 'You must never swim here,' she warned him. 'Not even in the shallow water.' She pointed to a fin, passing and repassing, just beyond the waves. 'Last winter a man in Bonita Shores was attacked by a shark. He survived but he went mad. My mother, when she was a little girl, was almost killed by a crocodile on the Caledon River. It gave her nightmares all her life. Thirty years later she would wake up nights shrieking. Do we ever escape from our nemeses?' She studied him gravely. 'Joe! Why are you always so far away?'

'I'm thinking. Sharks and crocodiles. Do you have a nemesis, Iraq?'

'Yes. Other people's nemeses are mine. My clients' ghouls give me nightmares too. But the deadliest of all nemeses is despair. I have to go to St. James this morning. I'll be back in the evening.'

Later, just before leaving, she put her hand on his cheek. 'Let me show you something,' she said.

She took a crystal goblet from a shelf, set it on a table.

She placed a silver teaspoon in it, stepped back, waited.

'How long have you been running?' she asked.

'All my life. What's that?'

The crystal was humming. The spoon rattled in the goblet.

'It's *you.* The whole room is vibrating with your panic. You're frightened to death. What are you afraid of, Joe? Tell me.'

'I can't talk about it.'

'Is it something inhuman?'

But he wouldn't answer. He went out on the terrace and smoked a cigar.

He spent the afternoon eating apples and reading a few chapters of *Tom Jones, Oliver Twist, Light in August, Madame Bovary.* He went down to the beach and watched the shark. Then he walked to Naples and had a cup of coffee and a slice of peach pie in a drive-in. On his way back a hick cop in a cruiser stopped him and wanted to know who he was and where he was staying. When Joe told him he immediately became polite and meek. He insisted on driving him back to the house.

By four o'clock she still hadn't returned. He paced restlessly through the pastel rooms, played a game of solitaire, tried to read again.

Then he realized why he was so irritated. He missed her. Her absence dug an enormous gap in the day. She mentioned clients. Clients? Who were they? Why were they depriving him of her – of her voice and legs, her smile, the marvellous convexes under her blouse, her hand touching him.

Hey! None of that! He was behaving like a jealous husband. She'd beguiled him. That would never do. Maybe he should leave now while she was gone – just split out in his corduroy trousers and leather sweater before the enchantment paralyzed him. *Go go go go Joe!*

He couldn't.

She came back at seven and his relief was so intense it left him numb.

'What was I saying about despair?' she asked, as if their conversation this morning hadn't been interrupted. 'The woman I went to see is a sad example. She spends all her time on the pier, watching the Sound. Her little son drowned there fifteen years ago and she keeps waiting for him to come swimming ashore, wading out of the water as if time had stopped.'

'How can *you* help her, Iraq?'

'I can bring him back for a while, to visit her.'

'Bring back the dead?'

'Oh, yes.'

'You mean a seance?' He was incredulous. 'No! Communicating with spirits and all that bullshit?'

'Yes,' she smiled. 'All that bullshit. A spirit can be conjured up, because it's already present. Listen …' she turned, held up her hand. 'Can you hear that?'

There was a muted sound out in the kitchen or in

one of the back rooms. It sounded like … what? As if twigs were scratching against the window panes.

'That's one.'

'A spirit?'

'Yes.'

'*Here?* You're kidding me!'

'Ever since you came into this house, it's been haunted. Do you want me to summon it?'

'No!'

They had dinner, then watched a comedy on TV. It was one of the Movie Star's pictures. Joe remembered them filming the exteriors at Santa Monica Airport and on the Mall. He began telling Iraq about his poker days at the 4 Straight, about Maxie and Roscoe the midget and Wheelchair and Mademoiselle Air France and the others.

'All right,' he said. 'Summon it.'

'A seance?'

'Sure. Why not?'

25

She lit a candle and placed it on the mantel. She hung a string of tiny bells on the edge of the bookcase. She opened a drawer, lifted out a curved stick.

'This belonged to Mantatisi, the Queen of the Wild Cat People. It's a witch-stick. She pointed it at her enemies and they were immediately demolished.'

'Is that where the expression "stick it to them" originated?'

'Are you aware that humor is a manifestation of fright?'

'I didn't know that, no.'

'Sit down and be silent.'

She turned off the lights and dropped to her knees in front of the fireplace.

He sat on the couch.

She tapped the stick on the hearth.

'Come forth,' she intoned. 'Show yourself. We are waiting for you. Come to me. Come to me.'

The bells tinkled.

'Come to me. Come to me.' Out in the kitchen, a chair scraped against the floor. 'Who is there?' she asked the shadows.

They waited.

She turned to him. 'It won't enter. You're holding it back.'

'No I'm not.'

'You are. Stop scoffing.'

She rapped the stick on the floor, on the leg of a table, on the wall.

'Come to me. Come to me. Come forth.'

The candle flickered. The bells danced on the string, chiming. The room's murk seemed to shift and ripple.

A figure came out of the kitchen and stood in the rim of light.

Joe started to rise. She stopped him with a gesture. He sat back, his heart pounding.

She addressed the form. 'Come closer. I can't see you.' It remained there, not moving. 'Who are you?'

It was a man, clothed in smoky opaqueness, stooped, limp, hesitant. He stepped forward out of the darkness.

Joe gasped.

'Do you know him?' Iraq whispered.

'It's my father.'

The spectre moved back into the dimness, then again into the candlelight. His eyes found Joe. His arms rose toward him.

Joe cowered against the couch.

'Don't be afraid,' Iraq murmured. 'He means you no harm.'

'Keep him away from me ...'

The hazy figure came across the room, filling the air

with a damp cold draught. Now it was almost upon him, its hands extended to grasp him.

Joe ran out to the terrace and down the steps to the beach.

She found him sitting in the sand, hiding his head in his arms.

'He's gone,' she said.

A trawler passed a mile offshore, covered with yellow lights, its horn blaring.

'Is he dead, Iraq?'

'Yes.'

'I didn't even know. How could I ...? He wrote a book on Brahms. I never even read it. I don't like Brahms.'

'The house is empty now.' She sat down beside him. 'No more ghosts.'

'The last time I saw him was in London.' He leaned against her. She slipped her arm around him. 'On my honeymoon. He used to say things like "Laurel and Hardy are contrapuntal." And he spoke awful French. *"C'est égal."* When Mom died he started going to a motel with one of his students. She had a boyfriend on the side, a senior named Porky. He didn't know that. *I* did. He married her, then she left him ...'

'But it isn't your father you're afraid of, is it?'

'No, of course not. Look! There's the fucking shark!'

The fin passed in the bright water, swooping toward them, coming into the waves, then disappearing into the iridescence.

'In those days I had a gift,' he said. 'It's called DOS.

Discoverer of Secrets. Sure, I knew all about Porky. And others. I knew lots of things. I knew who *she* was. I met her on Greenwood Avenue and I knew.'

'And she's the one you're running from?'

'Yes. She's looking for me. But I have one advantage. I can recognize her.'

'Who is she, Joe?'

'I'm freezing.'

'So am I. Let's go to bed.'

26

She came into his room just before sunrise. He was still awake. He watched as she pulled off her kimono and walked to the window. She stood for a moment, nude and gleaming, staring out at the Gulf. Then she came over to the bed.

'Forget it,' he said. 'I haven't had an erection since 1492 BC.'

'That's understandable. You're a pyschotic mess.'

'God! You're so black! You look like a panther standing on its hind legs. What a waste.'

'Waste not, want not.'

She lifted away the blanket and stretched out beside him. The moon painted her flesh crimson and jade. A passing cloud covered the window and she disappeared into carbon darkness.

'Who is she, Joe?'

Her breath blew over his chest, then his hips, then his thighs.

'She's blond. She has purple eyes. She dresses in mourning.'

His lips sipped at his loss, her tongue licked it, her mouth tasted it.

'Who is she?'

Deep within him, in a long disused railroad yard, a sleeping switchman woke with a start. Taken by surprise he quickly jerked levers and pushed buttons and turned rusty knobs. Cogwheels covered with cobwebs grated and turned, dusty lightbulbs glowed and blinked, ancient fuses cackled with sparks. Cables creaked.

And out of a ramshackle engine shed, rolling on shaky tracks, a vintage puffing locomotive appeared, its whistle wailing.

He couldn't believe it! He had a hard-on!

She tumbled over on her back, stretching out her arms, growling softly. He slipped atop her, his enormity pulling him in its wake, leading him into her.

And all the lost years, like a late crop, burst into fulfillment.

He still couldn't believe it. 'Did *I* do that?' he asked, awed by the accomplishment.

'I would say it was a mutual endeavor.'

'But it's never happened before ... not for ... for ... since ... what does it mean?'

'It means that your cure has begun. Taking off our clothes is part of the therapy. Now we must remove other obstacles.'

'First things first.' He reached for her again and she came against him, yielding, her zest as eager as his.

'But be careful,' her kiss hissed in his ear. 'You'll be arrested for speeding.'

In the weeks that followed they made love continuously. The bedroom became a place only for sleep and recuperation. Their sex was too urgent and spontaneous to wait for the discretion of night. Collisions took place in broad daylight, in the kitchen and on the terrace, in the laundry room and behind the carport.

He had only two failures, both due to over-reaction. But that didn't matter. Their pursuits involved all sorts of variations. A neighbour, a Dr. Blake, dropped in for an uninvited visit one afternoon and discovered them in the yard, in an oral duet in the grass. A mailman got the shock of his life, glancing through the front window and seeing them wrestling, naked, on the living room rug.

Joe was in no hurry now to go back to St. Petersburg. Iraq never brought up the question of money. She was fabulously wealthy. She was sometimes paid as much as a thousand dollars a 'sitting.' Rich clients came all the way from Miami and Jacksonville to consult her. One weekend she flew to Quebec to visit a haunted house in Ste-Brigitte-de-Laval. Her price: five grand.

She offered to buy him a car, but he refused. He had nowhere to go. When she wasn't there, he just walked up and down the coast or read all the books in her library. They went to restaurants in Naples and Pirate Harbor and Fort Myers. They spent a whole month in an expensive hotel on Lake Okeechobee.

They held another witch-stick seance. No apparition appeared.

The shark abandoned the beach. They could swim in the Gulf now.

From time to time, in moments when he was the most defenseless, usually after a prolonged bacchanal, she would ask him again, 'Who is she?' He still wouldn't answer. Then, in autumn, they had a visitor.

27

Joe drove the Triumph into Naples to return some cassettes. It was his last day of tranquility.

Coming back, he saw the two of them standing in front of the house, chatting like old friends.

Iraq was in her scandalous bikini, the other was disguised as a tourist, wearing black shorts, a black T-shirt, black glasses, a black straw bonnet, carrying a black sack.

Odd. They both looked ravishing. Tall and slim and lissome and sombre and blond.

He turned into a side road. His mind was suddenly submerged in glue. He couldn't think.

He found himself back in Naples. He pulled into the edge of a field and just sat there in the sun. He had to think … to plan … This was it. The end of everything. Iraq, the house, the feast, the haven. But he'd never expected it to last. It had to happen sooner or later.

So?

Why not just keep going north? Back to St. Augustine… no … not Augustine … St. … what the fuck was his name? St. Petersburg. Pick up the money-belt … leave the Triumph in a parking lot … catch a plane at

Clearwater … One thing was absolutely certain: he just couldn't sit here like an asshole doing nothing.

His friend the hick cop pulled up beside him in his cruiser.

'Anything wrong, Mr. Egan?'

'Hullo.'

'Lo. Anything wrong?'

'Mmm? No. Just letting the engine cool off.'

'Need any help?'

'No thanks.'

'Say you need any help?'

'No, I'm fine thanks.' Just go away, shitface, and do your Columbo routine somewhere else.

'Want me to have a look at it?'

Jesus! 'Don't bother. It's happened before.'

'Give my regards to Miss Iraq.'

'Right.'

'Have a nice day.'

'You too.'

He drove away finally. No … he wouldn't go north. The money was safe where it was. He could pick it up any time. He'd go south. But what the hell was south of here? Nothing. The fucking Everglades! He'd take *75 east.* To Fort Lauderdale. First he'd have to go to Golden Gate on the western end of the Alligator Alley highway.

He U-turned. The Triumph stalled.

It wouldn't start. He left it there and followed a path across the field. It led to a marsh. He tried to go back to the road. He couldn't find the path. It was gone. So was the field. He was in a soggy grove, littered with wrecked cars. How far had he come? His thoughts were gluey again. He sat down on a fender, lit a cigar, tried to relax.

So?

A blank. He couldn't think. Glue.

Losing the Triumph screwed up the whole program. He couldn't drive anywhere now. He'd have to hitch-hike. Or find a bus stop.

Anyway, he had to move. Fast. Now. His cigar tasted like rancid soot. He threw it away. His brain simply refused to operate. The sun blazed down, smothering him, baking the cars. He felt sleepy, drunk, breathless. The air was rotten and fetid. Indians used to live in these bogs.

Sergeant!

Sir?

We're in Siminole country, keep your eyes peeled.

Yes, sir.

Make sure you're not captured alive. These redskin devils feed prisoners to the gators.

Good god, Lieutenant! How hellish!

They're heartless savages.

Sir, what is that 1979 Chevvy doing here?

It must be the relic of some bygone age. Sic transit gloria mundi.

Something moved behind an overturned van. A broken headlight dropped to the ground.

He jumped to his feet as a long green alligator walked out of the wreckage just in front of him.

It looked at him with apricot eyes, opened its jaws. He climbed up on the roof of the Chevvy. The thing came after him, sliding up across the hood, its rows of yellow teeth as long as butcher knives. He jumped to the ground, ran through the maze of chassis. It followed him, guffawing at him, moving with unbelievable speed, skidding through the junk as if it had a hundred stubby legs.

Joe leaped up to the back of a wheelless truck. The gator tried to climb after him, heaving its awful wrinkled torso up against the cab, its hungry gullet yawning.

He dropped down to the other side, ran into a clearing. There was a shack in the distance. He started toward it when an old man in camouflage fatigues came barging out the door, aiming a shotgun at him.

'Get off my land, skumbag!' he yelled. And fired a barrel at him.

Joe dived into a gully as a tempest of buckshot ripped up the ground around him. He crawled along a slimy stream filled with tincans. Where was the fucking alligator? There it was! Jesus! Just behind him, thrashing down the embankment into the water. Its tail lashed at him, striking him across the shoulders, knocking him flat. He rolled away, his spine burning with pain. The shotgun's other barrel fired, dismembering a bush just beside him. The alligator stopped and looked around, grinning madly.

Joe scrambled out of the hollow, forcing his legs to hold him upright. A fence barred his way. He flopped over it.

He was back on the road.

A girl on a bike pedaled up to him. He stared at her. She looked familiar. She was wearing a bikini.

'Where on earth have you been?' Iraq asked. 'I've been looking all over for you.'

28

'What woman?'

'The woman you were talking to.'

'Oh, her. She was looking for Dr. Burk's house.'

An AAA mechanic recharged the Triumph's battery. They drove into North Naples and spent the rest of the afternoon sitting on the beach.

'She didn't ask for me?'

'For you? Of course not.'

'She didn't mention my name?'

'What is all this, Joe?' Then she laughed. 'Ah, I see. A blonde. With purple eyes. You think it was the sinister girl who's after you!'

'You got it.'

'Are you aware of how many blue-eyed blond honky nymphs there are in Florida? How can you tell them apart?'

'Don't laugh, Iraq.'

'It's going to rain. Let's go home.'

'I can't go back there.'

'Yes you can. Stop this foolishness and come on.'

'Do you think she saw me?'

The house was the same. There were no malignant vibrations. The hues and rhymes were in perfect balance.

Only the weather was vile. The wind rose, filling the air with flying sand, lifting the surf all the way to the terrace stairs.

They sat in the living room drinking calvados.

'Now,' she said. 'Tell me.'

So once again, for the third and last time in his life, he confessed everything. Now she and Father Patrick and mad Peggy-Sue were the only three people in the world to know his secret.

Her sole comment was a matter of fact. 'But you're not certain it was her.'

'I couldn't be mistaken. Neither could you.'

'Me?'

'You must have sensed something when you were talking to her. Something unnatural.'

She smiled. 'Unnatural? I did, yes.'

'What?'

'Looking at her, I thought, how lewd it would be, the two of us in bed together. Black and white. Her blond hair on my belly. Ah! My big lips on her pale breasts. And I wondered what she would taste like.'

'You're …' he was jolted. 'Iraq! Come on!'

'It's true. I was thoroughly aroused. That's when I began looking for you. I was in need of … reassurance.'

Her clothing dropped away. The feast spread before him once again. He'd thought he'd never see her body again. Now it was undulating wantonly before him, strolling into the bedroom, turning sinously, beckoning.

He followed the shining ebony flesh through the shadows.

Thunder woke him. Rain was crashing against the windows, lightning lit up the room.

He stood at the window, watching the storm. She was out there, he knew it. In the night and the wind, waiting in the rain, smiling at the thunder.

He prayed. O God, I never thanked you for giving me back my cock. I really appreciate it. Now just keep *her* away from me. Let me be the only one who doesn't have to endure the going hence, even as the coming hither.

Iraq stepped to his side, wrapped her arms around him.

'She's there,' he said.

'Certainly she is,' she stroked him delicately. 'She's always there. She always has been and she always will be. What of it? What are we expected to do, hide in a crypt until she finds us? Come back to bed, you dolt. If you have only five minutes to live, take advantage of the reprieve. Besides, I have some good news for you. I'm pregnant.'

In the morning came the bad news. The mailman told them that their neighbour, Dr. Burk, died yesterday.

29

He refused to leave the house. He peered out the windows all day, watching the road and the beach. Every time the doorbell rang, he'd sneak into the pantry and hide in a closet.

She tried to reason with him. The blonde was gone. Besides, she hadn't been looking for him but for the doctor.

'She found him and he's dead. And she left. Why would she stay?'

'She'd stay if she thought I was here.'

'But why would she think that, Joe?'

'Because her radar works too. Just like mine. When one of us is close, we both know it.'

She realized that arguing with him was pointless. She decided to get him away from Naples. She had a cabin on Gullivan Bay. They could go there for a while, until he got his nerve back.

She packed some provisions, closed the house and they left that night.

He insisted on making the trip locked in the Triumph's trunk.

She stopped under the setting moon and opened the trunk.

'All clear,' she said.

'Are we there?'

'Not yet. We just passed Naples Manor.'

He climbed out to the road, eyeing the darkness.

'She could be parked somewhere,' he mumbled, 'watching the road.'

'Never mind her. Tell me what you think of my announcement.'

They got back into the car, drove on.

'I think it's sensational, Iraq,' he was watching the empty highway behind them, 'except for one thing.'

'Oh? What's that?'

'I can never be a father or a husband. I can't possibly live any sort of normal life.'

'Well,' she squeezed his knee. 'I can always keep you locked up in the cellar and bring you out just for special occasions. For instance, for parenthood or for fucking every now and then. Is that abnormal enough for you?'

They both laughed. If he could laugh he was rallying. He made her stop the car again and they made love in a pasture. His craving was so intense and her rasps of pleasure so invigorating that he banished his fright in a maelstrom of pure lust.

The cabin was on an island two miles offshore. To cross the bay, she kept a motor launch at a wharf in Goodland, a high-powered Cariddi, painted orange and named 'Mantatisi.'

The sun was rising as they loaded their packs aboard and cast off.

It occurred to Joe abruptly that he was 'at sea'! He'd never been this far out on the water before. The illimited foggy landlessness stunned him. Where was the *earth?* Where were the trees and lampposts and mailboxes and the boulevards and bridges and ...?

And the haze! It was alive! He saw dragons in the mist, squids and krakens and ethereal goblins. Jesus! This was ghastly!

At the helm, Iraq pulled on a skipper's cap. 'I am the captain of this vessel,' she cried. 'And you are my crew! Our course is south-south-west to the Land of Bliss!'

He looked at her bleakly. 'I think I'm going to be sick.'

'You're not paying attention, sailor. Bliss! You'll spoil everything if you throw up!'

'Yeah right. How long will it take to get there?'

The deck rocked. He looked over the side. Was that a *fin?*

'Damn!' Her cap dropped overboard. She switched off the engine, threw one leg over the gunwale and leaned down to lift it out of the swell.

Then she was gone!

The sun broke through the clouds, washing away the livid gloom. He and the 'Mantatisi' were alone in the bay.

'Iraq!'

She wasn't there!

Then he saw the fin again. It cut past the bow, sank, reappeared aft, turning sharply.

Hands reached up out of the water and gripped the edge of the stern. He moved toward them …

White hands.

She surfaced just beneath him, glitteringly nude, her dripping blond hair hanging over her purple eyes. The skipper's cap was tilted on her head, the silver cat pendant was hanging from her lips.

He backed away from her.

She smiled, pointed to him.

His fist struck the throttle. The engine barked, the launch lunged forward.

He ran to the helm, looked back.

Far behind him her head looked like a melon floating in the bay.

30

He made it to Goodland simply by steering the bow toward the nearest shore. He killed the engine and drifted into the dock, slamming against it, splitting open the hull.

The Triumph was parked behind a boathouse, its key on a magnet under its fender.

He drove across the toll bridge to 41.

He passed the meadow where they'd made love last night. Normal couples called that 'a quick one.' It was part of the ordinary pleasures of being like everybody else. Well, no more of that.

What about her cabin? The Land of Bliss! He'd never see it! What was it like? He was sure it was a perfect place, with bright walls and clean floors and …

No more of that either.

He was doing eighty. He slowed to fifty.

He wouldn't think about the rest of it. Especially about her … his … their child. A child! God! That was beyond thought, out of reach of misery.

In fact, he wouldn't think of anything. That was a faculty that came naturally to him. Far far far down in the bottom of the chasm of cogitation was an even deeper cavity called Lacuna Pit. He'd just store all his inmost ponderings there, with his memories and his longings and his regrets. And shut the lid on them. Oh, they'd pop out every now and then, sure, to try to finish him off. But he could always put them back into their hole again – and again and again – until weariness dulled their sting.

It was getting hot. Already 80 degrees. A bright and cheerful day. For somebody.

By ten o'clock he was at the house. He sat in the driveway, wondering why he had come here. Then he remembered. She had a couple of hundred dollars in the drawer of her desk. He'd need that to buy gas.

The blinds were down, the rooms were already dark tombs. He found the money and went into the kitchen to drink a glass of water. And he saw her, standing in a corner of the hallway.

It was just a faint trace of her, barely discernible, like a rough sketch drawn on the wall with the faulty nib of a pen.

She moved into the living room. He followed her. He wasn't afraid. He tried to take her in his arms. But she eluded him, searching.

He knew what she was looking for. It was on the mantel. Her witch-stick. He lifted it down, showed it to her.

She pointed to the fireplace.

He lit some charcoal on the grate and burned it.

She went out to the terrace. He watched through the window as she floated across the beach into the sea.

Later, driving out of Naples, he saw the hick cop

standing by his cruiser on the crossroads. They both waved.

He didn't reach St. Petersburg until five o'clock. Too late to go to the bank. He checked into a hotel and slept like a log all night and all day, not waking until six in the evening. Too late again. He went to the movies and saw an Italian film, *La tragedia di un uome ridicolo.* He was in bed by eleven, reading *Newsweek.* All his griefs were safely stored in the Lacuna. He slept without dreams until dawn. He was at the bank when it opened and emptied his safe-deposit box. The money-belt was intact, stuffed with bills. More than enough to go anywhere and survive for a while.

Out in the parking lot he met Nellie.

Nothing ever ruffled her. She just drawled, 'Oh there you are hi.'

They had a drink at Spike's.

'I'm terribly sorry about what happened, Egan,' she said. 'Truly I am. I feel so guilty. Alice and I talked it over and we just had to admit that you couldn't possibly have been in cahoots with that wretched *salaud* Milch. We even phoned that club of yours in Los Angeles. They told us you were never disbarred for cheating. They said you even had a golden card, whatever that is. So I owe you how much? Do you remember?'

'Sure. Eight thousand. How is the abominable Alice?'

'Oh, she split out. She met some chick and they went off together. I haven't the faintest idea where she is. That's what I told the fuzz.'

'The fuzz?'

'She's been gone for over a year. She's now a missing person. She abandoned everything. Her clinic, her office, her apartment. She just took off.'

'No kidding!'

'I refuse to miss her. She was turning me into a rampant dyke.'

'Who was the chick?'

'Beats me. Someone insatiable, for sure. Alice could never get enough.'

He was rattled. A year ago? That would have been just about the time *she* showed up. 'How do the police know they left together?'

'They were seen at the airport, both of them, buying two one-way tickets to someplace.'

Well, he wouldn't bother to wonder about it. He dropped it into Lacuna Pit with the other incertitudes.

Before leaving, Nel unscrewed a bulb from the lamp on their table and slipped it into her pocket.

She drove him back to her loft. He took a last look at the Triumph, sitting forlornly in the bank's parking lot, then dumped it into the Lacuna too.

It was obvious enough why she'd brought him home. No sooner were they through the door when she began unzipping. But wasn't it too soon after … since …? If it had been anyone else beside Nellie, he would have bowed out. But her lilac scent and her cat face had always bewitched him, even when he was impotent.

'Do you want me to keep anything on?' she asked. 'Like – *oserais-je dire?* – my shoes?'

Iraq had always been indifferent to erotic fantasies.

She was too straightforward for such things. But he remembered the games he and Ada used to play. This gave him an inspiration. He felt himself stirring even as he thought about it.

'Nel, do you by any chance have a blond wig?'

'You bet.'

'And black stockings? And a black slip or something?'

'Oh, boy! What am I supposed to be playing? A widow?'

Already erect, he closed the curtains, undressed, hung his money-belt on an easel. And when she came toward him in the half-light, blond, feline, wearing her inky masquerade, his dismay and desire and mortal panic all conjoined, as they did, brutally, under the marijuana plants, coming together like molten welding.

31

He didn't know exactly what he'd accomplished by playing that charade, but Nellie was impressed. When he tried to say goodbye, she wouldn't hear of it. She was flying to Buffalo at midnight, she'd only be gone for a week. She wanted him to move into the loft until she returned. Or better still, why not come with her? She'd pay for the trip and deduct it from the money she owed him.

It sounded like a good idea, so they left together. She spent the whole flight talking about Alice.

'She arranged this exhibit. She owns a piece of the gallery. She's from Buffalo. Her daddy was a doctor too. He was completely bonkers. It must run in the family. He killed himself in the most atrocious way. He swallowed Nembutal pills then dug a hole in the garden and laid down in it and covered himself with dirt and just fell asleep. By the time they found him he was smothered. Isn't that baroque? *"Doctor, canst thou not minister to a mind diseased, pluck from the memory a rooted sorrow? Ah, therein the patient must minister to himself."* Did you ever memorize *Macbeth?* You promised me you would, remember? Alice's problem is …'

He dozed. When he woke she was still drawling.

'... she'd be outraged if she knew what happened this afternoon. She doesn't believe in hetero action. She thinks all men are skunks. She ... oh, look, there's Buffalo down there!'

They checked into the Humbolt Parkside. She was at her gallery most of the day, leaving him free to sit in the park or read in the public library, or to take long walks.

He avoided Lake Erie. It was too much like the Gulf. Even the smell of it spooked him. He'd never go out on the water again. Never! He'd keep away from boats and even beaches.

One afternoon they had lunch in a restaurant in Riverside Park and he couldn't eat because their window overlooked the Niagara.

'Egan, what ails you precisely?' she asked.

'I hate landlessness.'

'What in the world is that?'

'Haven't you ever read *Moby Dick?*'

'Naturally. I think.'

'Melville says water is terrifying because of its "landlessness."'

'Oh, stop. There's land on both sides of the river. You're just trying to be mystic.'

At night, in the darkness, she would don her blond hair and mourning veils and they would enact his morbid fantasy. The fierceness of his reaction to the ritual always exhilarated her and she began to refine her performances, playing the flux of his arousal with the skill of instinct, provoking him to passages of excitement that left them both drained.

'What are we up to?' she asked after one of these wild sessions. 'I'm not complaining, mind, just curious.'

What could he tell her? He had to invent a story. 'Remember Madam Manners, way back when, the General's widow?'

'Ah hah! Yes I do. A stately woman always in veils. And, *cela va sans dire,* you were in love with her when you were pubescent.'

'I used to watch her through the window at night,' he lied (Madam Manners! Jesus! That bat-faced hag!). 'I'd play with myself and come all over the rose bushes, scratching my dong on the thorns. Especially when she walked around the house bare-assed in her black stockings.'

'How quirky. If she only knew what she was missing. And me?'

'You?'

'Poor Nellie.'

'With Madam Manners I'm horny. With you I might feel inadequate.'

'What do you mean? Do you actually believe you've been fucking somebody else these last few days?'

(Somebody else indeed! Could he tell her about the Maiden of Dread? The Shark Goddess? The Angel of Going Hence? The Landlady of the Crypt? He was pointing the burning witch-stick at all of them.)

'"*Sometimes,*"' he quoted, '"*two see a cloud that's dragonish.*"'

'*Hamlet.*'

'Right.'

'You can't out-quote me, I know more Shakespeare

than you do. What's this one? *"What thou seest when thou dost wake, do it for thy true-love take."*'

'You got me.'

'*A Midsummer Night's Dream.* Was Madam Manners a blonde?'

She was supposed to go back to Florida at the end of the week. But on Saturday she disappeared.

He waited for her all night and all day Saturday. There was no way of getting in touch with her, he hadn't the faintest idea where the gallery was. He searched her luggage for an address. Jotted on the cover of her sketchpad he found a phone number with a Buffalo area code. He dialed it.

A machine answered.

'I'm out of town for the moment. Leave your number and I'll call you as soon as I return.'

It was the same voice that spoke to him – how many long years ago? – on Greenwood Avenue.

The voice from Somewhere Else.

32

This was something he couldn't dump into Lacuna Pit. It was too weird. So weird, in fact, that his curiosity was stronger than his apprehension. Anyway, if it were *her* voice, she was out of town, so he could rest easy for a while. He decided not to flee. Not yet.

He gave the number to the girl at the hotel's phone desk and asked her to find its listing. He slipped her a hundred dollars.

A half-hour later she gave him an address on Kensington Avenue.

It was a house, just across the street from Cleveland Park. A huge place, surrounded by a wall with a locked gate.

He followed an alley into the back of the property and climbed up on a dumpster. He could see the rear façade of the house from here. All the windows were shuttered. The grass in the yard was knee-deep, the hedges overgrown, paths invaded with weeds.

He pulled himself over the wall and dropped down to a driveway.

He moved through the thickets, crossed an eroded

flowerbed, passed a tumbledown arbor. The side windows too were covered with shutters. On the terrace were flowerpots filled with dead twigs. The paving everywhere was cracked and smeared. A sundial was heavy with vines.

He ran across the yard to one of the back windows. Its shutter was ajar. He pulled it open. He looked through the filthy pane and saw a long corridor, an archway at its extremity leading into a bare room.

The place was vacant, no doubt about it. No one had lived here for years.

So?

This was risky. Suppose somebody in one of the other houses saw him and called the cops? He'd be collared for trespassing. He should have an explanation ready. He heard a child call for help, for instance, and climbed over the wall to investigate. Or he was looking for his lost cat. Or he was a historian interested in vintage mansions. Or he was leading a cavalry patrol across the desert and came upon these ruins just by accident.

Sergeant, what do you suppose happened to the people who once lived in this abandoned homestead?

Apaches probably got them, Lieutenant. Or maybe they all starved to death when the crops failed.

Mmm. I'm not so sure. There's more here than meets the eye.

Sir! Do you mean to infer that the area is fraught with unfathomable phenomena beyond our comprehension?

Precisely.

Then I respectfully suggest we move on, Lieutenant,

before any harm comes to us. Sufficient unto the day is the evil thereof.

Then, somewhere in the house's dark corridor, a phone rang.

The machine answered. 'I'm out of town for the moment. Leave your number and I'll call you as soon as I return.' Click.

No, it wasn't her voice. Or was it? He wasn't as certain now as he was before. Was it or wasn't it? Balls!

Then another voice drawled, this one unmistakably familiar. 'Hi. Nellie Jarman again. This is the fifth time I've called and all I ever get is that fucking answering machine. I can't stay in Buffalo forever. Where are you?'

Nel came back to the hotel on Monday morning, looking mussed up and hungover. She'd been arrested for shop-lifting and had spent the weekend in the slammer.

'They put me in a cage,' she complained. 'With a ratpack of hookers smelling like old towels.' She stood under the shower, groaning. 'What a zoo. I've never felt more humiliated and befouled in my entire life. And for what? A scarf not worth twenty dollars. You should have heard the judge lecture me, the haughty asshole.'

'Why didn't you call me?'

'They only allowed me one call and I had to get in touch with somebody else.'

'Who?'

'Do you know what? One of those scurvy girls in the bullpen actually wanted to go down on me! Can you believe it! She kept pinching me, I'm covered with bruises, look!'

He waited patiently for her to finish her lamenting. But then she stretched out on the bed, nude and dripping, putting an end to all conversation. 'I need a good pronging,' she wailed. 'Forget about the foreplay and just ram it into me.'

He did. For the first time they made love without – as she called it – *une mise en scène.* It was better than fantasy, far more honest and unselfish. They both finished quickly and she slept, snoring blissfully.

He had to wait until she woke. Finally, well past noon, they ordered breakfast and he could question her.

'Where is this gallery of yours?'

'On Ferry Street. Why?'

'You'd better give me the number, so I'll know who to call if you get busted again.'

'That won't be necessary. The exhibit has been postponed. Which means I'll have to stick around for a while. What are your plans, Egan?'

'I tried that other number, but it was a dead end. My plans? I don't have any.'

'What other number?' she stared at him, lynx-eyed with surprise.

He showed her the pad.

'Ah yes,' she dismissed it with a careless wave of her fingers. 'That.'

'I got some woman on the answering machine.' Casually, 'Who is she?'

'Alice's mother.'

It was his turn to be taken by surprise. All he could say was, 'Oh.'

'I thought perhaps she might have heard from her. But she's never there when I call.'

He thought it over. It was an explanation – of sorts. Anyway, it was better than this endless fucking conjecture. Maybe he could drop the whole business into the Lacuna after all.

'I think I'll stick around for a while too,' he decided.

'Good.' She walked over to the bed. 'Let's do an encore.'

33

That voice tormented him. Of course, his childhood memory could have been faulty. After all these years, D minor could sound like D major. Not only that, but his constant anxiety could make any voice become sepulchral and threatening.

He called the number over and over again listening to the recording. It seemed to have a different pitch each time. He was certain it was her. Then, a second later, he was just as certain it wasn't.

Finally, he gave up, convinced he was being even more paranoid than usual.

But his unease continued, rising out of the Lacuna Pit like swamp-smoke from a bog.

Now that they had some free time together, Nellie took him on sketching expeditions all over Buffalo, filling her pads with drawings of monuments and squares and the lake and the river. They swam in the hotel pool and ate in out-of-the-way cafes. One night they saw *Desire Under the Elms* at Canisius College and the next night *Phèdre* at D'Youville. Both plays were about incest and this led to Nel confessing that Alice, when she was a child, had been raped by her father. She was pregnant at thirteen and had an abortion. That's why daddy buried himself alive.

'What about her mother?' he asked.

'What about her?'

'She has a lovely voice. She reminds me of someone.'

'All I know is that she's always out of town.'

They stopped playing their bedtime games. They made love calmly now, almost unconcernedly, as if they were adhering to a quota.

They were both restive. And expectant.

'What's happening, Nel?' he asked.

'Happening? What do you mean?'

But he didn't know what he meant. The passing days were like an airport lounge where they waited for a flight to be announced.

The announcement came two weeks later on Friday morning.

He was in the shower when the phone rang. When he came out of the bathroom he found her sitting on the edge of the bed, pale and innerved.

'That was the gallery,' she said. 'We're invited to a cocktail party this afternoon.'

'Is that what put you in shock?'

'Shock? I have an *épouventable* headache. I'm going to jog for a while.'

He went for a walk in the park and smoked a cigar. He was furious with himself. Why did everything have to be a Red Alert? Maybe she did have a headache. Maybe there was a cocktail party. Why should he doubt it? Where did this sense of creeping peril come from? Fuck all!

When in doubt, *run.* He was wearing his money-belt. He could jump in a cab and be at the airport in a half-hour. That was exactly what he was going to do.

He sat down on a bench instead.

If the next person who passed was a man, he'd stay. If it were a woman, he'd split.

He waited.

He puffed his cigar and blew a smoke ring – a perfect O. He sat there, admiring it as it floated away.

A little girl and boy came along the pathway, bouncing a basketball between them.

So much for that. When in doubt, *hover.*

At three o'clock they drove up Genesee Street and turned north on Harlem Road. She was driving and seemed to know where she was going. Obviously not to the gallery, Ferry Street was in the opposite direction.

'Where is this place, Nellie?'

'Not far.'

Then they were on Kensington Avenue. She stopped in front of a closed gate just across from the park.

The same closed gate in the same high wall he'd climbed over three weeks ago.

She blew the horn.

'Where are we?'

'J'en sais rien.' She shrugged and lit a cigarette. 'This is the address I was given.'

'Don't you know who lives here?'

'No.'

'I do.'

She looked at him, for just an instant letting her nervousness slip past her nonchalance. 'You do? Who?'

'Alice's mother.'

She laughed. 'Alice's mother is dead, Egan.' She blew the horn again.

'That's not what you told me.'

'I lied. Sorry about that, old buddy.'

'Then whose number have you been calling?' She didn't answer. 'Who have you been calling, Nel?'

'Somebody else.'

'Somebody who told you to bring me here?'

'Yes.' She was astonished. 'How did you know that?'

'She told you to bring me to Buffalo and to keep me here until she got in touch with you. Is that it?'

'You've known that all this time?'

'No. Not really. But why, Nellie, why? What will she give you in exchange for me?'

'Alice.'

The gate swung open, its hinges squeaking. He could see the house now, at the top of the driveway, all its windows unshuttered, the panes glinting.

So.

She was in there, waiting for him ... welcoming him, bidding him enter. *The time has come, Joe. I've waited long enough.*

The front door opened. She came out of the hallway and stood on the steps.

He leaped out of the car and ran down the block.

34

A week later he telephoned Nellie in Tampa.

'Egan! You rascal, where are you?'

She was herself again, cool and drawling. A good sign.

'Back in LA,' he lied. 'What happened with Alice?'

'All's well that ends well. She lost some weight, but that's a plus. That obnoxious woman put her on a diet.'

'You mean she let her go?'

'Of course. I kept my end of the bargain, she had to keep hers. It wasn't my fault you flew the coop at the last minute. But I'm glad you did.'

'Tell me, Nel, why did you have to go all the way to Buffalo to close the deal?'

'Because of Alice's house. That's where that blond bitch had been keeping her all these months. Locked up in the cellar! Can you imagine that! No one ever thought of looking for her there.'

He refused to imagine it. That would lead to an inevitable crack-up.

'She came to see me and told me that if you ever showed up in Florida again, I was to take you directly there and call that number. What could I do, Egan?'

God Almighty! It had all been planned, ever since she lost trace of him in Tampa. How many other traps had she set for him?

'Egan?'

'It's okay, Nel. All is forgiven.'

'But you have a lot of explaining to do, buddy. First of all, just who the hell is she?'

He hung up.

He wasn't in LA. He was seventy-five miles from Buffalo, in Rochester, living in a motel on Bay Street.

His hair was died white, he carried a cane and walked with a fake limp and was registered under an assumed name. He stayed there for three weeks then, when he became too comfortable in the role he was playing and actually began to feel elderly and crippled, he moved across the state to Albany. He threw away the cane and washed out the dye.

His confidence was returning, he was sleeping more or less soundly again, the Lacuna wasn't erupting.

It was difficult, trying not to think about Alice, locked up in that cellar for – how long? – a year? With *her* for a jailer. What a grisly nightmare! Going to all that elaborate mischief, just to catch him off-guard. Jesus! In fact, the whole scheme was an act of desperation. Capturing him had become her obsession and she was ready to go to any extremes to get her hands on him. What would she try next? Where? When? How?

Stop.

This was as far as he permitted his thoughts to delve.

Anyway, aside from that, things were no worse than usual. He was still free and alive. That's all that mattered.

He remained in the Albany area. The most off-the-beaten-track place he could find was a three hundred dollars a month vacation cottage on the bank of the Mohawk River, not far from Niskayuna. The landlord was a Mr. Leopold, who owned an antique shop on River Road. Joe told him he was a writer, doing a book on – he picked a name at random – Talleyrand.

His new home was just large enough to contain one room, a kitchen and a shower. It was called 'The Nook.'

He lived there for four years.

He hiked and read and bought groceries and watched hundreds of cassettes on his rented VCR.

A stray cat who visited him every now and again was his only friend. When he first showed up he was reading Zola's Rougon-Macquart saga, so he called him Emile.

Time meant nothing to him. One day it was snowing, the next it was August. He grew a beard, shaved it off, grew it again. When his hair grew to his shoulders he shaved his skull too. He stopped smoking cigars and began again six months later. He read *War and Peace* twice and, just for the hell of it, memorized *Macbeth.*

The river frightened him, but he forced himself to take endless walks along its bank, exorcizing the water. Eventually he could wander all the way to Mohawk View and back.

Mr. Leopold found all this highly equivocal. He'd drop by occasionally to try to be neighborly and to pry. He was in his sixties, chubby and flighty and a nuisance and gay.

'You're an enigma, Mr. Grayson,' he'd say, chirping

playfully. (Grayson was the name Joe was using these days. Lionel Grayson.) 'But sooner or later I'll unmask you.' A wink. 'Get to the bottom of you, as it were.'

'If I drop my trousers,' Joe would reply with weary coquetry, 'will you lower the rent?'

And Mr. Leopold would chuckle with delight and shake a finger at him. 'I never mix business with pleasure. And if the sheriff should ever hear you talk like that he'd run you out of town. This is an uptight community. Oh, by the by, how's the book coming?'

But it wasn't Mr. Leopold, or the sheriff, who put an end to his vacation. It was a bruiser named Frank, who showed up during the fourth year. He was over six feet tall, weighed two hundred pounds, and was Leopold's boyfriend.

Leopold brought him to the cottage and used him as bait, hoping to interest Joe in troilism. He was like a proud farmer exhibiting a prize bull.

'Frank knows the ropes,' he bragged. 'You can't fool him. He's been there and, hah, back.' And he added mysteriously. 'He doesn't pull his punches.'

Frank just grinned stupidly and fingered his fly.

He began loitering around 'The Nook,' inviting Joe to go fishing with him or volunteering to chop his firewood, making no effort whatever to conceal his mating-dance swish.

When this didn't work, he started playing rough. He'd grab Joe in an armlock, hold him tightly and rub against him.

'This is how the cons do it,' he sniggered. 'Ever been in the joint, Grayson baby?'

'Let me go, Frank.'

'I could break your fucking arm like this. Or pull it out of your shoulder. Don't you wish you had muscles like me?'

'Let me go.'

'Leo says you did time probably. That's why you're so freaky. What was you in for? Molesting kids?'

'Let me go.'

'Make me.'

He finally released him and swaggered away, fondling himself.

He was back the next day. And the next and the next, his kidding around becoming more and more painful.

'You wanna know what we call dudes like you, Lionel? PHTG. Playing hard to get. As soon as I have you really warmed up, you'll be begging for it.'

Joe didn't know how to deal with this kind of bullying. The asshole was just too gigantic to fight. And too numb-headed to talk to.

One afternoon he found him in the cottage, taking a shower.

'Howdy, baby!' He aimed a cucumber-sized hard-on at him. 'RWA! Ready Willing and Able!'

Joe picked up a towel and snapped it at his dong. Frank howled, then came out of the shower with insane eyes, ready to kill.

Joe fled. Frank chased him through the woods, bare-assed, all the way to the road, baying with rage.

Joe spent the rest of the day hiding in a nearby quarry, wondering how he'd ever gotten himself into this asinine situation and trying to figure out how he could put a stop to it. There was only one answer to that. A full retreat. He couldn't take any more of this bullshit. In fact, Leopold too was becoming a pain in the ass. And the woods and the Mohawk and 'The Nook' were beginning to close around him like a penal colony.

Time to go.

Are the troopers prepared to move out, Sergeant?

All saddled up, Lieutenant.

We'll leave at sundown.

I'll miss this campsite, sir. Heaven's breath smells wooingly here, the air is delicate and recommends itself to our gentle senses.

Quite so. But we can't stay here forever, Sarge. Besides, one stopping place is as good as another. And who knows! Our next bivouac might be even better.

At twilight he came out of the quarry and snuck through the woods. He got as far as the river.

Over on the opposite bank, a hundred yards away, walking along the crest of a high slope, was a tiny figure in black, wearing a blond crown.

An instant later she vanished, absorbed by the trees.

No – he was sure there was no one there. Absolutely positive. It had been a trick of the eye … just a … (You're kidding yourself. It's *her.*) No it isn't … a mirage … an illusion … (You saw her.) I didn't see her. I thought I saw her. I always think I see her. Everywhere. (Look again.) I am looking. (She's over there in the trees.) No … she isn't! (She'll come over here now and find you.) The beheld takes any shape the beholder invents! Sometimes we see a cloud that's dragonish! (You have maybe a half-hour to haul ass! Go! go! go!)

He ran to the cottage. The front door was wide open. The money-belt should have been on the floor, under Leopold's fake Napoleon III buffet ... but it wasn't. It was gone! Fuck all!

Frank stepped out of the closet, holding it aloft. 'Is this what you're looking for, sweetie?' he waved it at him. 'Where'd you get all this bread? There's enough here to go to the Bahamas on our honeymoon!' He grabbed him by the shirt, shook him. 'You hurt my cock, motherfucker! Now you're going to kiss it to make it better!' He backed him into the wall, hit him with the belt. 'You been begging for it, now you're going to get it!' At this point Emile the cat hopped off the buffet and landed on his shoulders. Frank screeched and jumped aside.

Joe picked up the poker from the fireplace and swung it at his thick bulging neck. He was dead before he hit the floor.

35

He locked the cabin, put the key in the mailbox, dragged Frank's body to the river and dropped it into the current. Emile followed him, rubbing against his legs, then trotted off into the night.

He walked toward Niskayuna, hurrying, putting as much distance as possible between himself and 'The Nook.'

Exit Lionel Grayson.

He'd take a taxi to Schenectady and ...

Somebody was following him.

He jumped into a wayside ditch as a car came into view behind him – slowly, hardly moving, its lights out. A black Cad, shining in the moonlight like a big phosphorescent cockroach.

It began to rain.

It passed him, taking an eternity to drive by, the driver invisible behind the darkened windows.

Suddenly, going to Niskayuna and Schenectady didn't seem like such a good idea.

He ran off in the opposite direction, east, toward Verday. Albany! *Run! run! run!* He'd take a bus to Albany, spend the night there and tomorrow get the hell out of New York and go ... Anywhere! He turned south on the Shaker Road, toward the airport. He already missed Emile. Las Vegas maybe. He'd go to Las Vegas, sure. It was time to get back into the poker money. Poker! Frank! Christ! Into Lacuna Pit with all that! *'Double double toil and trouble!'* What did he have to show for these four years except *Macbeth?* And a murder. That poor simpleton didn't have to die. He should have just rolled on the floor, unconscious, then woken later with a bump on his head. But no ... he had to blow it! Now there'd be an investigation, an inquest, an autopsy. Christ Almighty! The poker! It was still in his pocket!

He pulled it out and buried it in a deep hole in the muddy ground. Just like Alice's father.

The Cad appeared again, in front of him now, coming north from the airport.

He stepped behind a tree and it passed, still blacked out and slow moving.

He didn't spend the night in Albany. He caught a midnight Greyhound to Newark, New Jersey. He slept all the way, waking only once, as the bus was speeding through Kingston. He saw a sign in a field: *'80 MORE SHOPPING DAYS TILL CHRISTMAS!'* Ho! ho! ho!

His money-belt was only half-empty, but to affront Vegas he wanted a full treasury. For that he needed his old savings account in the Raleigh bank. He flew there the next day.

He closed his account and put the money in his belt.

He walked around the city, smoking a cigar, looking for forgotten doorways and malls and bookstores.

Wade Avenue, Pullen Park, Oberlin Road. Peace Street! He looked up at the windows of his apartment. Who was living there now? What color was the wallpaper? Was Ada still working for Esor? Was she still in Raleigh?

She was.

She came out of the entranceway, carrying a briefcase, wearing a tan raincoat and a white beret. And glasses.

Holy Moses! It was really and truly Ada!

He was across the street, standing behind a row of parked cars. She couldn't see him. There was a man with her and – Jesus Christ! – a little boy!

The three of them walked up the block. So did he, keeping covered.

She'd remarried naturally. And she'd kept the apartment … sure. Four rooms and two baths. Giving that up would have been silly. And she'd had her dream child. A beautiful kid! How old was he? Three or four. Right. After seven years the absent husband is legally non-existent, so Mr. Right No. 2 proposed.

Beloved Ada, will you be my bride?

Yes, Amos. I thought you'd never ask.

Who was he? A big guy, as burly as Frank. But handsome, clean-cut, civilized. An executive. Squash, golf, tennis. The understanding type.

Not tonight, darling. I have a headache.

Yes, precious. I understand.

Wouldn't it be super-nifty if life were like a novel and she'd married his father … No, he was dead. Or – surprise! – Leopold. Or the midget, what was his name – Roscoe – at the 4 Straight Club. Fiction was easier to handle than reality. Reality was agonizing. He felt as if he'd been stabbed with a saber. He was trembling … reeling … babbling … Ada! This was incredible! She looked superb! He'd never seen her hair that long … and her legs … and … She leaned over to say something to the boy and the agile swerve of her spine and her waist made his groin tighten in response. God! No more of that!

The boy was laughing. What had she told him? *Do you see that funny-looking man over there? He could have been your daddy. But he ran away from poor mommy years and years ago because he's a psychopath. He jumps on buses and planes and trains that don't go anywhere. He sleeps in motels with brown walls and hides in dumpsters, squealing like a rat. And not only that, he's also the infamous Mohawk Valley Poker Killer!*

'Hullo, Joe,' a voice behind him said.

36

A chubby young man in a turtleneck sweater smiled at him.

'Are you talking to me?'

'You're Joe Egan, aren't you?'

'Nope, sorry.'

'Sure you are. And that lady across the street is your ex-wife.'

'What lady?'

He walked away. He came down St. Mary's to the Civic Center, turned into Martin Street. He looked back. Chubby was a half-block behind him.

A cop! The guy had to be a cop! This was a fucking stakeout!

He crossed Chavis Park. Students from Shaw and lunch-hour office workers were sitting on the lawns and benches in the October sunshine. But the crowd wasn't dense enough to hide in.

Why? Why would they have Ada staked-out?

This is an ambush, Sergeant! The Apaches were waiting here for us!

They sure were! We're surrounded!

But how did they know we'd be coming through here?

They're cunning devils, Lieutenant. They figured that sooner or later we might pass this way.

Right. He wasn't a cop. He was a private operator hired to keep Ada under round-the-clock surveillance, in case he came back to Peace Street to visit her.

It was the only possible explanation.

It was another one of *her* traps. Nellie in Tampa, Ada in Raleigh. And he walked right into it like an idiot! She'd have a fix on him now.

He cut back to Martin Street, then up to New Bern.

Was Chubby working alone? Probably. It would be a one-man operation. He had to keep him busy ... don't give him time to make a phone call to bring in a back-up team ... past the Museum ... past Pullen Park ... up Brooks Avenue ...

Chubby was right behind him all the way.

He had to lose him. How? There just wasn't anywhere to hide. The whole city was an immense pitfall.

He went back to his bank. In through the front, out through the rear into the parking lot, then off into Whitaker Mill.

No good. The plump shithead was still glued to him.

He tried again at his old bookstore. In through the front, out through the side exit, up the block – fast! – across the street, into an alley. Now he was back on Peace Street.

So was Chubby.

This was pointless. A pro would be familiar with these clumsy tricks. He had to surprise him with something unpredictable. He needed *a* ... what was it called? An edge ... a coign of vantage.

He entered a sporting goods mart on Greenwood. He bought a bicycle for a hundred and fifteen dollars.

He pedaled up Greenwood, turned east into Lake Boone, then south into Dixie. The bike was light, swift, easy to handle.

Better than a car. He rolled along a sidewalk into a one-way street, turned into a narrow byway behind Meredith College.

He stopped, looked back.

Nobody!

So. Now where? He had to get out of Raleigh, away from this snare. What about Durham? It was only twenty-five miles from here. Or would it be better to head into the countryside? Into Wake County … no way! Wake? A name like that was a no-no if ever there was one!

Another cyclist rolled out of a lane just in front of him.

It was Chubby.

Joe spun around and pedaled away from him.

Now began a crazy bike race from one end of North Raleigh to the other, up and down hills, through the parkways, across bridges and parking lots, around and around, in and out of every winding street and pathway between Blue Ridge Road and North Boulevard.

Chubby was always just yards behind him, as tireless as a robot, hunched over his handlebars, his fat legs pumping effortlessly.

Joe just couldn't out-distance him.

Then, on Six Forks Road, he passed a girl jogging.

Blond, shapely, running as lithely as a gazelle. He had only a glimpse of her as he pedaled by, then she veered into a driveway.

No … it couldn't be *her* … Chubby hadn't had time to notify her. And besides … all blonds looked alike.

How can you tell them apart? Who said that? Iraq.

There was a hospital around here somewhere … acres and acres of grounds … he'd lose the bastard there maybe …

There it was!

He dismounted, picked up his bike and carried it under a chain barrier into the grounds of Community Hospital.

Seeing him do this, Chubby made his first mistake. He braked too hard, twisting his front wheel. He was pitched out of the saddle and sent sprawling into a gutter.

Joe remounted, coasted off into an area that exited on Wake Forest Road. He had his … what was it called? His coign of vantage. A small one … but it might give him time enough to find an escape hatch.

He crossed the Crabtree, dismounted again, wheeled the bike into the woodland.

He dropped to the ground on the bank of the creek, breathing like a kettle, his thighs throbbing.

Are you hit bad, Lieutenant?

Just a scratch, Sarge. It'll be all right.

I think we lost him.

Good. He's a Pinkerton agent, Sergeant. She hired him to find me. That woman is unbelievable!

What woman, sir?

I'm not supposed to talk about her. Top secret.
That blond girl we saw running back there?
No, that was just a jogger.

'Egan!'

He jumped. Chubby was on the other side of the creek, limping down the bank, puffing and pink-faced. 'You Yankee sonofabitch!' he bawled. 'I'm goin to kick the shit outer you!'

He splashed into the water and waded toward him, shaking his fist in the air like a Communist marching in a demonstration.

'You think you're pretty damn smart, don't yuh! Well, I'm goin to show you what we do to wiseass little pricks like you in North Carolina!' He sank to his knees in the mucky creek bed, then to his hips, then to his shoulders. He screamed and went under all the way, the water bubbling over him.

Joe just sat there watching him, bleary-eyed. He tried to rise, but his legs wouldn't hold him up. He dragged himself across the bank, hugged the trunk of a tree, grabbed a branch, managed to get to his feet. He picked up his bicycle, lugged it back to the road.

37

He left the bike in an alley and took a taxi to the airport. He flew to Charleston, West Virginia. It was the only flight he could get on without a reservation.

He stayed in bed in a motel for three days, reading Livy's *War With Hannibal.*

When he was feeling better he still wasn't ready for Vegas. There was something about going there that bothered him. He couldn't analyze it, he was too exhausted.

He flew to Chicago, then to Boston, then to Cedar Rapids. He'd just sit in the airport lounges, reading, have lunch or breakfast or dinner, then take off on whatever flight was available.

A security guard in Cedar Rapids put a stop to this nonsense. He kept an eye on him for a while, finally asked to see his ticket.

'My wife has our tickets,' Joe told him. 'And she's late, as usual. Have I done something illegal, officer?'

'We got an APB on a guy,' the guard said. 'You fit the description.' But he wasn't too sure. 'Uhh sort of.'

'What's he wanted for? Can I buy you a drink?'

'No, sir. I'm on duty. Murder suspect. Supposed to've kilt some nigger female in Florida.'

'Do you want to see my ID or what?'

'No, that's okay.'

'Florida. I've never been there.'

'I was in Miami for two weeks last year. City's full of kikes. They go down there to retire. Must be a couple million of them.'

They chatted about Hitler and baseball and football and tardy wives and airline bookings. And that was the end of it. Thank God! If the asshole had made an issue of looking at his ID it would have been Catastropheville!

Iraq! Christ! She was hidden so far down in Lacuna Pit that he'd forgotten that he might be considered a suspect in her death. A murder rap! Balls!

Well, it was a big country. There were hideaways everywhere. They'd never find him. An APB was a joke. He was no worse off than before. No worse off than poor Hannibal, wandering around Italy with his elephants. 'There was nothing he could call his own, nothing to look forward to beyond his daily plunder.' That was okay. Sufficient unto the day was the plunder thereof.

Of course he'd have to avoid sharp-eyed cops, like the security goon, but that was easy enough. It was just a matter of not attracting attention. Loitering around airports had been a brainless mistake. He wouldn't do that again. Starting right now.

Pretending to take a stroll around the lounge, he slipped outside and jumped into a bus that was going to Dubuque.

He got off at a place called Cascade and remained there a week, living in an awful rooming house. He told the landlady he was interested in opening a barbershop.

He spent days looking at dusty vacant stores, jotting figures in a notebook, talking to rustic merchants. It kept him occupied and he met some friendly folks, including the mayor, the sheriff, the president of the Chamber of Commerce. The latter was also a used-car dealer and sold him a '79 Mercury Zephyr for only two hundred dollars. He drove to an even bleaker town nearby called Otter Creek and spent another week playing the same farce.

What he was really doing was growing a mustache.

In November he went to Las Vegas.

He checked into the first inconspicuous hotel he saw, the Shoshone on Suzanna Street. After taking a nap and a shower, he went to a coffee shop next door for lunch.

Sitting at a table, slobbering down a salad, was Milch. 'If you're lookin for a hot poker game,' he snarled, 'it'll cost you a hundred bucks.'

Joe shrugged. Better to get back on the merry-go-round right away. He'd been postponing it long enough.

They went to a shabby bungalow on Rochelle Avenue. There was an all-night-all-day game in the living room. The players were mostly local louts, acting tough and grim, the way they thought Vegas card pros should behave. He saw one of them slip Milch a tip. So that was how the little creep was living these days, steering tourists into hustling parlors.

Joe played until six, winning and losing practically nothing, then he had enough. Before he left, the dealer, doing his hard-guy act, told him he'd have to contribute to the Nevada Veterans' Fund. He pointed to a basket filled with twenties. Joe dropped a quarter into it.

Milch was waiting for him outside. 'The real action starts round midnight,' he said. 'The other night a high roller dropped eight grand in one pot.'

'The guy in the slot was cheating.'

'Chester! What're you sayin! Chester cheatin! You're goofy! Geeze, I hope you didn't say nothin. He'll clobber me for bringin you.'

'So long, Milch, I'd invite you to dinner, but your table manners are too primitive.'

'Fuck you! Read my lips! Fuck you!'

He took a walk along the Strip, merging into the crowds, smoking a cigar, feeling uneasy. He went into the Desert Inn and wandered around, played the slot machines, bought a shirt in a gift shop, watched a dice game for a while.

There were thousands of people coming and going. This was the ideal city for becoming invisible. Why was he jittery?

He went back to the Shoshone. But he couldn't sleep.

He got up and went down to the lobby. Milch was there, in drag, wearing one of his ugly get-ups.

He followed Joe out to the parking lot.

'Remember those two crazy broads in Florida?'

But Joe didn't want to talk about Nellie and Alice. 'Go away, Milch,' he said.

'I was back there last Easter. I seen them. One of them anyway. The other one's in a convent.'

Joe turned to him, jolted. 'Which one?'

'The doctor broad. She had a crack-up, the nutty broad. She found God. Her girlfriend told me. Nel. What a pair of fucked-up broads. Where you goin?'

Joe got into the Zephyr and drove off.

A convent! Poor Alice! She must have known who had kept her in the cellar all those months. She surely figured out who she was. Just as Peggy-Sue had. One went mad, the other became a nun.

He drove north, past Spring Mountain Road. Fuck Vegas. He'd go to Reno or Tahoe.

He pulled over to the curb. Spring Mountain Road. That sounded familiar. It had a hopeful echo, bringing back soothing memories. Memories of what? Earrings. Another road, another car. Real estate. *A nifty apartment on Spring Mountain Road not far from the Frontier Hotel.*

He found her address in a phone book. It was a small, modern building, ultra-chic, behind a high fence. He climbed over it and went into the entrance. Her name was on a mailbox. The apartment was on the ground floor, in the back, in a jungle of shrubbery by the pool.

He tapped on the window with a dime.

A light went on. 'Who the hell's that?' she yelled.

'It's me. Rudolf the Randy Rapist.'

'Oh, brother!' She opened the window. Mickey Mouse's huge round head smiled at him on the front of her nightshirt. She was wearing a patch on her breast. *'Joe!'*

'Hi, Maxie.'

'You have a mustache!'

38

'What a year this has been! I lost a hundred grand in March. I just couldn't win a single hand. It was like playing poker with calling cards. Then all of a sudden I started cleaning up like crazy. Everything turned to gold. Blackjack, basketball games, horse races, roulette. Then I smashed up my car on the Santa Monica Freeway. A stoned truckdriver cut in front of me doing ninety. I was in the hospital for three weeks. My blood pressure ran amuck. So now I'm back on Catapres-TTS patches. Once a week. Then my husband died. My ex-husband. Now you show up ... wow!'

They'd spent the rest of the night in the kitchen, drinking coffee and eating scrambled eggs. Now they were lying beside her pool in the boiling morning sun. He was smoking a cigar and yawning. She wore a see-through bathing suit and was sipping orange juice. She looked like an advertisement for a vacation in Tahiti.

'What have you been doing? Milch told me he saw you in Tampa. You were mixed up with a couple of dykes.'

'Yes. Nellie and Alice. A fun couple.'

'Milch has gone completely off the rails. I ran into him in Century City and he was wearing his dress and wig in broad daylight. At night he's a horrifying enough sight in drag, but in the sunlight he is positively repugnant. Have you been lucky at least?'

'I've had my ups and downs.'

He was becoming uncomfortably erect. Her body purred to him. He didn't want to talk. He wanted her to take him in her oily arms and absorb him. But he was too shy to tell her. But she noticed his longing and reached over and touched him gently.

'Is this one of your ups? Goodness gracious! Have you been taking pills or something?'

'Nope. I'm just glad to see you.'

'Really? But weren't you always glad to see me?'

'Sure. But … you know … like a sister.'

'Oh brother!' Her fingers walked up and down his thighs. 'I don't know like if I can deal with this. It's too like overwhelming.'

'I'm so tired, Maxie,' he put his face against her shoulder. The heat of her skin burned his cheek. 'And lonely. When I close my eyes I see sharks in the ocean and swamps filled with alligators. And when I try to sleep, ghouls come looking for me.'

'So what can I do for you, pal?' she whispered.

'Hide me.'

They went into the bedroom. Her nakedness flowed around him like a waterfall of warm balm, soothing his bruises, cleansing his pain, sanctifying him. He fell asleep inside her, hidden and secure, the world locked out, all his frightful dragons far away.

In the afternoon she eased out from under him and left the apartment. He woke at four.

The first thing he saw was the wallpaper. It was a montage of newspaper headlines. He opened the blinds and spent an hour reading them, digesting the history of mankind in nibbles *'"The di is cast!" says J. Caesar', 'Edward II Dethroned for Homosexuality,' 'Lincoln elected by Landslide,' 'Pope Pius VII Excommunicates Napoleon,' 'Lenin Dies,' 'President Johnson Signs Civil Rights Act,' 'Allies invade France.'*

He found 218 BC. *'Hannibal crosses the Alps!'* (He wondered if she had been there too, riding on an elephant at the battle of Cannae. But he was feeling so revived that this thought didn't even depress him.)

He took a shower and examined his mustache. It looked ridiculous. He'd have to shave it off one of these days. His hair was getting long again too. Time for a clip. What had he done with that shirt he'd bought yesterday at the Desert Inn? It was still in the Zephyr.

He realized that this concern for his appearance meant that he was starting to think sanely again. Good. Maybe he was in for another spell of peace and tranquility. He needed it. Christ, how he needed it. And Maxie too … he needed her.

He read some more headlines *'Mongols sack Baghdad,' 'Mary Queen of Scots Beheaded,' 'Cromwell Defeats Royalists at Naseby,' 'Paris Mobs Storm Bastille.'*

He went out to the pool to take a swim. But he couldn't quite make it. He kept imagining that the water was thick with snakes.

Maxie phoned at six, inviting him to the Gold Mine for dinner.

She was in one of the cocktail lounges, drinking bourbon, still misty-eyed with tenderness.

'I just cannot get over it,' she said. 'We actually screwed. I feel all tingly and gooey!'

It was true. She was transformed. Her face glowed like a lamp and her body was vibrating with lusty signals.

'Let's finish up here fast and go back to the sack.'

'Finish up what?'

'A friend of my husband flew in from New York last night. He wants to have dinner with me and reminisce.'

'How did your husband die, Maxie?'

'He fell into the Mohawk River and drowned.'

He wasn't certain he'd heard her. A waiter came over to the table to take their order and she introduced them. 'Bob, this is Joe, an old pal of mine. Treat him VIP.'

'You got it, Max.'

Joe tried to unwrap a cigar and almost broke it in two.

'Drowned?' His shoulders were aching, he crouched, unable to sit up straight. 'In the Mohawk …'

'Yeah, they found him floating past Schenectady or someplace. The sheriff there says maybe somebody gave him a shove. They're looking for the guy he was fooling around with. The big poker games are upstairs. Suite 707. Very private. I'll get you in.'

'What was his name?'

'The waiter? Bob. Oh, you mean the guy they're looking for. I don't know.'

'No, I mean your husband.'

'Frank Hearn. Why? Oh hey!' She pointed. 'That must be him.'

Standing on the other side of the lounge talking to Bob was a man in a dapper tux.

It was Leopold.

39

He made it to the men's room without throwing up and once there, enclosed in a booth, his stomach stopped quaking.

He began to laugh.

A joke. Maxie and Frank. What mad choreographer had invented that nutty tarantella? No! It had to be a joke.

He came out of the John and looked into the bar. Maxie was smiling, ordering more drinks. Leopold was posing simpering, playing with his lapels. Wow! There they were, 'reminiscing.' Chatting about poor Frank and Lionel Grayson. Wow. He'd fled all the way to Niskayuna and spent four years there holed-up in 'The Nook' like a hermit – for nothing. He might just as well have come directly to Vegas and stood in a spotlight on the stage of Caesar's Palace singing 'I Did It My Way.'

He left the Gold Mine, slinking away like a thief. He went to the Desert Inn, escaping into the crowds. So much for his spell of tranquility! He was famished. He ate a ham sandwich and a banana split. Three well-dressed hookers tried to pick him up. No thanks, girls, not interested. I'm saving myself for the widow of the gentleman I'd brained with a poker then dunked in the river. Wow! What a magnificent shambles his life was. He'd like to have a look at the blueprint that designed him. What a diagram that must be. The draftsman had probably been stoned. It was ten o'clock. He put some quarters into the slots. *Frank.* Jesus! That bullying creep married to Maxie. It was after midnight in North Carolina. Ada was asleep beside her understanding husband. *'The Thane of Fife had a wife, where is she now?'*

'Can I help you, sir?'

Oh, no! Another security guard. Ape-faced, bulging in his uniform, ears as big as wings.

'Are these machines really honest, friend? Tell me truly.'

'Yes sir. Guaranteed?'

'I never win.'

'Just keep trying.'

'I always do that.'

'That's the spirit.'

He escaped and went to the Riviera. Then to the Sands. He still felt like throwing up. Old one-eyed Hannibal must have gone through this nightmare, trapped in Southern Italy, lurching from Bruttum to Lucania, then back again, surrounded, hunted, enwebbed. He'd have to read that book again. Sentences kept popping into his head. 'Four statues dripped blood in Feronia.' 'In Targuinii a pig was born with a human face.' 'Seventy Numidians were seized and their hands chopped off.' 'Mice ate the gold in Jupiter's Temple.' And those groovy Roman names. Publius Sempronius Tuditanus, Titus Quinctius Crispinus, Quintus Fabius Centumalus.

He did throw up finally, in an alley somewhere behind the MGM.

Maxie was still awake when he came back to the apartment. She was in the bedroom, taking off her bra, changing her patch. That's exactly what she'd been doing when he first saw her, in Atlanta, millenniums ago. It gave him a this-is-where-I-came-in feeling.

'Sorry,' he said. 'I felt too putrid to have dinner.'

'You didn't miss anything. The guy's as gay as can be. Real boring.'

'I'm going to take a bath and shave off my mustache.'

'Good idea. It looks like a disguise.'

'I hope you're not going to wear your Mickey Mouse nightgown.'

'I'm not going to wear anything, pal. Hurry up.'

They made love slumberingly, revolving together as nimbly as dancers. He closed his eyes. Then it was morning, the sun shining on the headlines on the walls. They came together again, leisurely.

'Number 3!' she crooned. 'And that's only the beginning, folks!'

'All that time lost,' she sighed. 'All those nights we slept alone on Eleventh Street. Your room's still there, by the way, with your books and everything.'

'*The Brothers K!* I never finished it.'

They were in the kitchen, having breakfast. It was already 85 degrees and they were both nude.

'Leopold told me … that's his name. Leopold. He's an antique dealer. He and Frank were living together. And this other guy, Grayson … that's the one they're looking for. Lionel Grayson. I'm going to put some more sugar on my cornflakes. The hell with calories.'

'What did he tell you, Maxie?'

'Grayson was renting this place. A house Leopold owns. He was writing a book. And he just skidaddled and left all his stuff behind. Like you did in LA. Hundreds of books. Do you want some more coffee? And sweaters and pants and shoes. That's why the sheriff got suspicious.'

'Lionel Grayson, yeah. That name sounds familiar. I think I read one of his novels. He writes horror stories.'

'He was a raging fag.'

'What?'

'He raped Leopold every time he came to collect the rent. Then when he met Frank he went wild. "Your husband's muscles," Leopold said, "were Michelangeloic." His very words. Michelangeloic. Can you imagine those three rural homos loose in the woods, playing leapfrog with each other. It must have been odious. How Frank ever got that far down the drain I'll never know. He was straight when I married him.'

'If you ask me ...' Joe was seething with rage. Leopold! The lying vicious little nerd! 'If you ask me, I'd say Leopold probably killed them both in a fit of mean-queen jealousy. Grayson is in the river too.'

Maxie was taken aback by this. 'Do you really think so?'

'Does this Leopold fellow strike you as being a wholesome, trustworthy, law-abiding citizen?'

'After two drinks he tried to put the make on Bob the waiter. And come to think of it ... hey! Oh, brother!

Do you know what he said? "When I found the two of them in bed together" – he was talking about Grayson and Frank – "I was so angry I could have strangled them."'

In bed together! How do you like that! The miserable prick! 'Well, there you are.'

'You can judge for yourself. He has a suitcase filled with stuff that belonged to Frank. He's bringing it around this morning.'

'Here? He's coming here?'

40

It was nine-twenty. Leopold arrived at half-past. Joe didn't even have time to dress and leave. When the doorbell rang he ran into the bedroom. Maxie paid no attention to these eccentricities, she just shrugged.

He could hear them, prattling in the living room.

'Oh, what a cozy place! Is that a Boston rocker? And what do I see over there! That sideboard! Permit me to have a closer look if I may. Yes, by George. Honest to goodness eighteenth century. Worth a fortune. You're lucky I'm on vacation or I'd haggle you into selling it. I can only stay two minutes. I have a tennis appointment at ten-fifteen. This heat is dire. And, naturally, the air-conditioner in my car isn't working.'

Joe sat down on the floor. Was this really happening? Was that really Leopold's voice whining and wailing out there? Or was it all just feverish recall and self-torment? By what right had this insignificant dork come prancing out of the past to torture him!

Now they were looking through the late Frank's belongings.

'This was his favorite jacket. A birthday present from yours truly. I don't know why he kept all these hankies. He never used them. That roughneck blowing his nose in a handkerchief! Never! This is a souvenir. I bought it for him in a crazy little store in Atlantic City. See? You pull the string and the arms and legs move. He loved it. I'm sure these socks have never been laundered. Postcards. Magazines. His Dodgers' cap. The dear boy adored baseball. It's all just junk, but I thought you might … I miss him so. He was sweet chap. Oh, please don't cry!'

Joe listened, repelled. They were talking about sweet Frank as if he were St. Francis of Assisi and his departure from this world would be a great loss to mankind. The sadistic fink deserved a slower death. Boiled in oil maybe, or drawn and quartered.

'Rest assured, Mrs. Hearn, that scoundrel Grayson will be caught eventually and punished … I beg your pardon? You mean …? Both of them? Well. I never thought of that. Yes, it's a possibility, I suppose. May I use your bathroom?'

Joe rolled under the bed and watched Leopold's shoes walk through the doorway and across the rug into the bathroom. He was wearing green moccasins and white socks. Maxie's slippers came in a moment later and stopped beside the bureau. She was probably wondering where he was. She retreated. The moccasins came out of the bathroom and strolled over to the wall.

'Oh, how cute! *"British Army Burns Washington, DC," "U.S. Jets Bomb North Vietnam."* How utterly!

"Aristotle Dies," "Lee Defeated at Gettysburg," "Theodore Roosevelt Elected President." I'm admiring your wallpaper, Mrs. Hearn! It's ducky!' He went back out into the living room. 'You know, there's another possibility. I never told the sheriff, because it slipped my mind. On the afternoon Frank disappeared, it was about four o'clock, a woman came to my shop looking for him.'

What was he saying? Joe crawled out from under the bed and scrambled over to the door.

'Very smartly dressed, insolent, New York City-ish. "Frank Hearn," she said, "where is he?" Not even bothering to be polite, snapping at me as if I were a domestic. Well, that was the last straw. I was still fit to be tied over all that nasty hankpanky with Frank and Grayson, so out of sheer pique, I gave her a false address. I told her he lived on the other side of the river. That was terribly rude of me, I know, I know, but I was devastated.'

Joe sat down on the edge of the bed. Her! That blond apparition on the bank of the Mohawk had been real! She'd come for Frank!

'I shall! I certainly shall! I'll see the sheriff the moment I get back to Niskayuna. Heavens! I have to dash off. You can tell that person hiding under the bed he can come out now ...'

'You were right,' Maxie said. 'Did you hear him. As soon as I mentioned the possibility of Grayson being dead too, he began squirming and running to the John. Because it automatically makes him suspect number one. So straight away, hah! He had to invent somebody else showing up out of nowhere the day Frankie died, hah!'

'Out of nowhere, you said it.'

'An insolent woman from New York. Brother!'

'Maybe it's true though. Maybe there was a woman.'

'Hah! I'm going to phone that sheriff in what's-it-called and tell him what I think.'

He checked out of the Shoshone that afternoon and moved into the apartment. In the evening she took him to Suite 707 at the Gold Mine and introduced him to several of the players.

They were a high-grade group, as exclusive as a board of directors. There was no nonsense here. Just poker. Levity was tolerated but frowned upon, as were drugs and drunkenness, loud voices and IOUs. Cheating was unheard of, a capital offense.

Joe had no idea who these people were and couldn't care less. The glacial atmosphere suited him, their grave stodginess was congenial. He was accepted without question because Maxie vouched for him. If he goofed she would be responsible. But he wouldn't goof. He didn't want to kid around, he wanted to win pots.

They played all night and he lost only four hands. They watched him closely, looking for a bamboozle, but his playing was faultless. Maxie, as aware as he was of their suspicion, tried to turn it into a joke. After one big win she quipped, 'He must be marking the cards or something.'

The others cringed. Making light of so taboo a subject was a definite no-no.

But by dawn they were finally convinced he was simply skillful and lucky, virtues they could cope with. They'd get their money back sooner or later. In the meantime he was invited to play again whenever he liked.

'You've been accepted,' Maxie said when they were downstairs. They had an expensive breakfast in the dining room then went home to bed.

That afternoon, Leopold found him.

41

He took the Zephyr to a garage on Paradise Road for a tune-up. He parked in the back of the lot and was walking toward the office when Leopold came out of a car rental agency on the next corner. He was wearing Bermuda shorts, a safari jacket and a tam-o'shanter. They were a half-block apart, face to face.

Joe pretended he didn't see him, wandered casually into an alley. Then he ran as fast as he could toward the next street.

Leopold came trotting after him, shouting and waving his arms.

Get behind them rocks, Lieutenant. I'll cover you.

Thanks anyway, Sergeant, but you'd better come with me. You don't want to be caught out here in the open either.

Yes, sir.

There was a shopping center at the end of the block.

He hid there for an hour, drifting in and out of the stores, watching the entrances.

Who was that bozo, sir?

A tenderfoot I used to know in civilian life. He can ruin me because of a mishap I was involved in back East.

What are you going to do about it, Lieutenant?

There's nothing I can do. Except pray.

The situation is in the lap of the gods as they say. Is that what you mean?

Exactly.

He took a taxi back to Mountain View.

'Leopold just called,' Maxie told him. 'He says he saw Grayson on Paradise Road.'

'Who is he kidding?'

'He's desperate. He has to convince everybody that Grayson is still alive. Not only that, but he wants me to report it to the police. Which makes me an accessory.'

'Leopold is becoming a monumental pain in the ass. How long is he going to be in Vegas?'

'He was on his way to the airport when he phoned.'

She climbed out of the pool and he took her by the hand and led her into the apartment.

'Again?' she laughed. 'This cannot go on. Poker all night and poke her all day. We'll be basket cases!'

They didn't bother with the bed. They made love against the wall, surrounded by the headlines.

On Christmas Eve they went to the dull show at the Sahara, then walked around the Strip with the hordes of holiday visitors.

They met Milch, in drag, cruising the hotels. They invited him to have a Yuletide drink with them.

'I don't want your charity!' he sneered. 'Just give some bread so's I can get back in the game.'

'What about your long-going hoodoo?' Maxie asked.

'I got your long-going hoodoo dangling! Get me into 707 and I'll wipe out those motherfuckers!'

'They'd never let you into 707, you know that.'

'They let him in!' he snarled at Joe. 'What's so special about him?'

Maxie was furious. 'For Christ's sake,' she yelled. Look at you! You're a god-damned disgrace! Why do you behave like this? Are you retarded or what?'

She walked away.

'Rah! rah!' he barked after her, thumbing his nose. 'Up yours! Up yours!' Then he grabbed Joe and dragged him into a doorway. 'Your goose is cooked, wise guy!' he smirked. 'All I gotta do is say the word. One word from me and your goose is cooked.'

'What are you talking about?'

'What're you talkin about,' he mimicked him. 'What're you talkin about. You know what I'm talkin about, jerk. I'm talkin about your blond girlfriend that's what I'm talkin about.'

Las Vegas suddenly became icy. Joe froze.

Milch went capering off across the street, skipping and giggling like a tipsy matron. On the opposite pavement he turned, lifted his skirt, kicked his short legs like a cancan dancer. 'Tra-la-la-la!' he sang. 'Tra-la-la-la-la!'

Now Joe knew why coming to Vegas had bothered him. There were people here who knew him, opponents from thousands of games who could put the finger on him. Naturally, she would stake them out too, just as she had Nellie and Ada. He cursed himself for not having been aware of this in time. Now it was too late.

She'd gotten to Milch. And maybe even to Maxie!

'Maxie.'

'What?'

It was Christmas afternoon. They'd slept till eleven and were in the living room now, sitting by the tree, listening to carols on the radio.

'Remember, years ago, that blond woman you met in Des Moines, Utah, the one who was asking about me?'

'Des Moines is in Iowa.'

'Wherever.'

'No.' She was reading the sports page of the *LA Times*. 'I loathe football. It's so uncouth and crude. Yes. The Vogue blond. Sure.'

'Have you ever seen her again?'

'Yeah, as a matter of fact. In Indianapolis, about three years ago. Did I tell you I have a penthouse in Indianapolis?'

'I think so.'

'Bigger than this place, five bedrooms.'

'Where did you see her? In the street or what?'

'Right there in front of my high rise on English Avenue. She said, "Hi, Maxie." No she didn't. What she said was, she lowered her voice, "Good evening, Mrs. Hearn, do you live here?" Very formal and dignified. Like the head waiter at Ma Maison. At first I couldn't remember who she was. Then I recognized her. "Yeah I live here," I said. And I asked her if she was still trying to get in touch with you.'

'And what did she say to that?' As if he didn't know!

'She said yeah she was. And I said, "So am I." Imagine running into her *twice!* Is she ...'

The phone rang.

He went into the kitchen and drank a glass of

grapefruit juice. He wasn't worried about Milch. The little fucker was too conniving to blow the whistle on him. He'd try something else first, just to see how far he could push his advantage. Blackmail probably. A few grand now. Later a few more. He wasn't used to having the upper hand. He'd play the situation for all it was worth.

'I know,' Maxie was saying in the other room. 'He told me that too. I didn't believe him. Grayson in Las Vegas hah! It sounded just too convenient. Okay, we'll be in touch.' She hung up and ran into the kitchen. 'That was the sheriff in Niskayuna. Leopold's been arrested for Frank's murder.'

42

'Did Maxie tell you about our accident?' Milch asked.

'Yeah,' Joe said. 'On the San Diego Freeway.'

'The Santa Monica Freeway. We was goin to a bridge game in Pasadena.'

'She didn't tell me you were with her.'

'Well I was.' He was immediately on the defensive, whimpering peevishly. 'I didn't have a car. I still don't. Whenever I gotta go somewhere I gotta bum a ride. Is that something to be ashamed of? Huh?'

They were in the coffee shop of the Hilton. He was wearing a wrinkled and stained yellow suit and a cowboy hat. But he didn't look any more outlandish than the rest of the tourists having lunch.

'She rammed into a truck, the dumb bitch.' He chewed his steak, open-mouthed, making clicking noises. 'I was all banged up. I was in extensive care for a month.'

'Use your napkin, Milch. Wipe your chin.'

'Then one night …' he closed one eye, grimacing, going into an unpleasant flashback. 'In the hospital …' the memory confused him. 'I woke up and she was standing there, bending over me. She was blue.'

'Blue?'

'Because of the lights. Blue. I thought it was one of the nurses. But …' he scowled, the memory still fluid. 'She said … that's when I knew it wasn't one of the nurses. When she talked, I knew all their voices. They was always yappin at me.'

'Yeah. So?'

'She said, "You're not goin to die, Milch. Just tell me where Joe Egan is."'

Joe crossed his legs under the table. His feet were cold. He looked out the window. A woman passed with a large police dog on a leash. Then three men carrying golf bags came by. Then several children. Then a group of tennis players. Sometimes he felt as if he belonged to another race. Another species.

'Then what?'

'She left. And about a week after I got outta the hospital I gotta telegram. Just a phone number with a 213 code. I called up a couple a times. Always an answerin machine.'

'Did you leave a message?'

'Yeah. I said I didn't know where you was.'

'Good.' He picked up his cup of coffee to warm his hands. 'Now listen carefully, Milch.'

'I'm all ears.'

'This woman is dangerous. I don't want to have anything to do with her. I don't want you to have anything to do with her either. Just call that number again and tell her you still don't know where I am.'

'In a pig's ass! Why should I cover for you?'

'You're not listening, Milch. Dangerous, I said. Just as dangerous for you as she is for me.'

'What's she got on you anyhow?'

'Never mind that. Just stay out of it.'

'Maybe I will and maybe I won't.' He was impressed, his face quivering with indecision. There was something about the whole thing – the blue woman, the telegram, the oddness of it all – that made him leery. 'What's in it for me?'

'Maxie's going to get you into Suite 707, for old time's sake. If you promise not to make a fool of yourself.'

'I know how to be just as phony as anybody else!'

'And I'm going to give you some money to bail you out of your misery.'

'How much?'

There it was! His beady eyes were brimming with greed. He was back in the game.

Maxie had some trouble getting him into the suite, but her clout was considerable and they finally admitted him. He played poker there for the first time on New Year's Eve. Aside from some sneering and snarling, he behaved himself very well. He played professionally, breaking no rules, keeping his voice down, drinking only one scotch. And at midnight he wished everyone a happy new year almost graciously. His hosts found nothing to object to.

Joe and Maxie celebrated January the 1st by driving into the desert to watch the sun rise.

An eagle dropped out of the pale orange sky and perched for just an instant on the hood of the car, then flew away. According to Titus Livius, this was a Roman omen.

Another year. He refused to count them. They made no sense to him. They were like centuries or decades, too massive to contemplate. A calendar was as incomprehensible as a heliographic chart. Only his days and nights mattered. One more morning, one more twilight, an infinity of moments. Time was an illusion.

But it was nice having someone to share the illusion. He knew that Maxie was a trap, tempting him deeper and deeper into her body, into his need for her. But he couldn't help himself. She was too appeasing, too satisfying. He'd run away from her once, he wondered if he could do it again if he had to. He was like Hannibal's army in Capua. Hot baths and soft beds and dancing girls were sapping his will, making him inert and shiftless. When the time came for flight, he might sink.

In February he became a silent partner in one of her deals. He had no interest in real estate, but she kept insisting, horrified to discover that all his winnings were in his money-belt. So he finally invested fifty grand.

He gave Milch two thousand a month and paid his rent.

In March a mob smashed into the Niskayuna jail and tried to lynch Leopold.

The poker continued, either in 707 or some other hotel. They usually played twice a week.

Maxie changed her patch every Saturday.

The winter passed.

This is turning into a long furlough, Sergeant.

We need the rest, Lieutenant.

That we do.

Maybe we can stay here forever.

That would be fine. But just the same, keep the horses saddled up so we'll be able to ride out in the twinkling of a jiffy.

Nothing happened until June.

Milch was doing well, playing with surprising restraint, winning small but steadily. He had money in the bank these days and for the first time in his life was out of the red. Joe hadn't seen him in drag since Christmas. He was considering cutting his allowance.

But the morning he met him in the Palace bar, he was a nervous wreck.

'She called up last night,' he bleated. 'I got her on my answering machine. You wanna hear it?'

Joe went with him to his grubby hotel room and they played the message.

'Mr. Milch, you know who this is. I'm still very anxious to find Joe Egan and I'm still waiting for you to tell me where he is.'

Nothing else. Joe felt the old familiar queasiness flooding him with bile, numbing him, making him abject.

'I'm scared,' Milch whimpered. 'Why am I so scared?'

'She's frightening. If a black samba or a shark could talk, they'd sound like her.'

'What'll you do?'

'Nothing. Absolutely nothing. Fuck her!'

43

Maxie had to go to Indianapolis to see a lawyer. He went with her.

The warning signals began to flash as soon as they arrived at Weir Cook Airport. A blind man tripped over Maxie's valise. A woman fell on an escalator just in front of them. Their taxi driver was drunk.

The penthouse was worst of all. It was a superb duplex, with high ceilings and wide walls and a dining room that sat twenty people. But it was forty floors high, surrounded by outer space! Vertigo was lurking behind every window. He made her close all the curtains.

'You get used to it,' she said. 'But if there's a fire, so long!'

He shuddered. A fire. Jesus. He began looking for escape routes. There weren't any. Just the stairs and a private elevator.

'Oh, don't be so squeamish!' she cried. 'Doesn't the altitude make you horny?'

They made love on a round waterbed in one of the rooms. On the nightstand was the ultimate omen. A framed photo of Frank.

Later in the afternoon, while she was at her lawyer's office, he wandered through the warren of rooms, feeling exposed and defenseless. Why? Why would Indianapolis be more hazardous than anywhere else?

He thought it over, becoming more and more convinced that staying here could be a disaster. She knew Maxie's address. She'd already been here once before, right out there on English Avenue, reconnoitering the terrain. What if she came back again today or tonight or tomorrow just to see if anyone was home?

He left the building and checked into a hotel on State Avenue. Then he hid a getaway valise in a locker at the bus terminal.

He took a long walk and didn't get back to the penthouse until seven.

Maxie's lawyer invited them to dinner. Then they went to a party in a house on Oliver Street. Everyone there was snorting coke and listening to old Harry James records.

He went out to the back yard and sat down wearily on the steps. His Uncle Joe had been a Harry James fan. When he went off to war he left a whole box of records with Mom. Joe had been three years old when he left. He vaguely remembered VE Day and VJ Day. People cheering and cars blowing their horns and Dad hanging a flag out the window.

He lit a cigar and watched two guys dancing together in the driveway.

How was he going to tell Maxie he didn't want to spend the night on her rooftop? Problems problems.

Being a couple was difficult. If he were younger, he'd just run. But he didn't want to lose her. She was surely the very last chance he had not to be alone in the world. His caution these days wasn't as strong as his dread of solitude. That would probably doom him. We all think there's safety in togetherness. Like those two chorus boys capering gayly in the moonlight. They thought they were protected by their homo fellowship. But that wouldn't save them. The Mafia dacoit had his Family, the Catholic his Church, the Jew his tribe, Lou Gehrig his baseball team. And Uncle Joe his 8th Air Force. But in the end everyone dies his own lonely death, as solitary as a mangy old wolf crawling through the frozen woods.

'Joe!'

That sounded like Ada, calling to him in the blizzard. Better to be dead than on the torture of the mind to lie in restless ecstasy. Act Three, Scene Two.

'Wake up!'

Christ! He couldn't open his eyes! The lids were stuck!

A hand tapped him on the top of the head. He woke with a start. Maxie and the two gay dancers were standing around him. She introduced them. He didn't catch their names. X and X. They both had beards and were wearing gold chains around their necks.

'They want to play poker,' she said. 'Or would you rather stay here. There's an orgy getting underway.'

'No orgy please.' He pulled himself to his feet. 'Poker by all means ...' He was still clutching his cigar. 'Balls! Look! I burned a hole in my pants!'

The four of them drove back to the penthouse in a

Bentley, Maxie and X and X gossiping about people he'd never heard of. She'd evidently been living in Indianapolis off and on for years and was as much at home here as everywhere else. They talked about him as if he weren't present.

'A business associate,' she said. 'We've been buddies for years. He's the only man I've ever known who never tried to rip me off. For a while he couldn't get it up. I cured him of that. Now we fuck all the time. We'll probably get married. I was always terrified at the idea of growing old all by myself, an elderly hag with lots of real estate and nobody to talk to. That'll never happen now, thank God. Well always have each other. We're partners.'

Joe was touched. She had everything all worked out in advance, like a flight plan. She didn't know her partner was the Flying Dutchman.

They played all night and he won twenty-six thousand. At sunrise he lost the last game when he was dealt a pair of aces and a pair of eights. A deadman's hand.

He ran.

She was outside, sitting on a bench on English Avenue, waiting for him.

44

After a long ride on three different buses, he ended up in Lafayette, Indiana. From there he flew to San Francisco.

He lived in Oakland for six months, then moved north to El Cerrito.

He went back to Vegas only once. His Zephyr wasn't in the parking lot. It had been towed away. Maxie refused to let him into the apartment. When he met her at the Cafe de Paris she wouldn't even speak to him. She sent an envelope to his hotel. It contained a cashier's check for $50,000.

So much for partnerships.

Bob, the waiter at the Gold Mine, told him Milch was gone. Nobody knew where. Or cared.

Flying back to San Francisco, he read in *Time* that Leopold had been found not guilty.

He moved south to Alameda, then north to Piedmont, then west to Emeryville.

He bought a secondhand Monza V8 and spent most of his time driving around the shore of the Bay, going nowhere.

That's how he discovered the Golden Gate Track.

He'd never been interested in racing. He'd gone to Hollywood Park with Maxie a few times when they were living in Santa Monica, but the imponderables of horses had always baffled him.

Now he found himself fascinated by them. Especially their names. Green Past, Golden Hawk, Steeple Dancer, Lady Ruby, Magic Pie, Drugstore, Moon Knife.

He was there every day, betting once in a while, winning and losing, but mostly just watching the races and prowling through the crowds.

On the 4th of July he ran into Milch. He was in drag, standing by the paddock, eating a hot dog.

They had a drink in the bar.

'I had to get out-out-outta Vegas,' he stammered. 'She kept callin me up. Every day. Every night.' He looked hideous, his turtle's face streaked with lipstick, his eyelids painted violet, his wig lopsided. And enunciating had become a major problem. 'I-I-I told her you was livin with Maxie. I had to to to get her off my back. Then she called me again. "He is no longer with Maxie," she said. "Where is he now?" And she-s-she said, "Don't forget our pact, Mr. Milch." What did she mean by that? Pact pact? What pact?'

'Remember when she came to see you in the hospital? She told you you weren't going to die.'

'Yeah.'

'She meant you'd stay alive until you found me.'

'Huh?'

'That was the pact.'

'What're you talkin about?'

'Don't you know who she is, Milch?'

'Just some crazy no-good broad. The world's full o'them. See? A couple of drinks and I can speak great. Well, when I run into her again I'm goin to tell her you're here. Fuck this ramshit.'

'I hope for your sake, asshole, that you never see her again.'

'I seen her last Saturday. In Berkeley, on Ashby Avenue. She was on a bus. She waved to me.'

An hour later Joe was on a plane, flying to Seattle.

He spent the night there, then flew, first to Phoenix to have a look at the Paradise Race Track there, then, two weeks later, to Arkansas, to the Oaklawn Track in Hot Springs.

This sudden obsession with tracks wasn't really serious, but it gave him something else to do besides playing poker and climbing up the walls.

Next came the Keystone and Liberty Bell races in Philadelphia. Then on to Hazel Park in Detroit. This was the briefest of visits. On the third night there he saw a poster announcing a concert at the Cultural Center. Brahms' *Requiem!* He fled to the airport and flew to West Virginia.

He spent a whole month hanging around Wheeling Downs. He began betting more heavily, trying to put some savor into these crazy trips. He studied the Racing Form. He bought an expensive pair of field glasses. He talked to bookies and jockeys and touts and trainers. The secrets of horseracing still eluded him. The only killing he ever made was on an outsider named Kismet. 30 to 1. He pocketed ten thousand dollars.

When the turf crowds began migrating to Churchill Downs in Louisville, he followed them like a lemming.

He left the glasses behind in his hotel room.

45

'Oh, by the way, I got a postcard from Leopold,' Maxie said. 'He's in Paris. He beat the rap, the maggot! I miss you, Joe, honestly I really do. But ... Oh, by the way again ...' she unbuttoned her shirt and showed him her bosom. 'I stopped wearing Catapres patches again. My blood pressure is nifty-peachy. You're just too unstable. Instability is so tiresome and maddening. I want to lead a quiet life, without bumps.'

In Louisville, the first person he'd seen when he came into the lobby of the Floyd-Taylor Hotel was little Roscoe, the dwarf from the 4 Straight Club.

'Your Majesty the King!' he shouted. 'Noblesse oblige!' He spelled it. 'N-o-b-l-e-s-s-e-o-b-l-i-g-e! The taproom's this way, follow me!'

He was retired now, in his nineties – at least – tinier and more buffoonish than ever, resembling a fossilized pygmy.

'The club's closed down,' he lamented. 'All boarded-up. The roof caving in. Everybody gone away, scattered to the four winds. All those wonderful people. Nothing left but nostalgia and *Heimweh*. H-e-i-m-w-r-no!-w-e-h. Did you know Maxie's here?'

He called up her room and she came downstairs and joined them in the bar.

'Hey!' she cried. 'This looks like a reunion of the Santa Monica goon squad!'

The three of them had lunch in a pub called 'The Merry Jarvey.' It was packed with racing fans and as usual she knew everybody there.

'If you come back,' she told Joe, 'you'll have to promise me you'll try to behave normally for a change, instead of freaking out all the time. I just can't deal with your goofiness any more.'

It was an ultimatum and an invitation. He was tempted to accept. It would give him a few days' rest. He could always sneak away later. But no … that wouldn't be fair to her. She deserved better than that.

'I can't come back, Maxie.'

'Speaking of goofiness,' Roscoe said, 'do you recall our dear friend the Movie Star? He cracked up. Coke and pills and scotch. The last picture he made was never released. They say he was stoned in every scene, babbling like a madman, tripping over the decor. Then he tried to cut off his wife's nose with a razor. She had him committed, poor fellow.'

'Why can't you come back?' Maxie asked.

'No wait,' Roscoe snapped his minuscule fingers. 'It was that sailorboy. Remember him? The one who was building a yacht. *His* wife had *him* committed. He went bankrupt and sold his yacht then started acting ding-dong. Like throwing flowerplants out the window and setting fire to the furniture and such. The Movie Star's in Hawaii, I think.'

'Oh, brother,' Maxie sighed. 'There's Milch.'

It was Milch indeed, dressed as a male today, wearing his cowboy hat and his stained and wrinkled yellow suit. He was drunk.

'Louisville phooeyville!' he yelled. 'All the races are fixed!' He came wobbling over to their table.

'I dropped a grand already and I only been here two days. Is it true, Roscoe, you gotta normal-sized cock?'

'Keep your voice down, you vulgar motherfucker!' Roscoe was blushing. 'I've knocked bigger dudes than you on their ass for talking to me like that! Drunken sot!'

'I gotta drink,' Milch whined. 'Otherwise I start stutterin like I was retarded. It's called ophasier.' He sneered at Joe. 'We gotta have a talk, smartass.'

'Aphasia,' Roscoe corrected him. 'A-p-h-a-s-i-a.'

'Shit,' Maxie groaned. 'S-h-i-t.'

Joe lit a cigar. What an odd quartette they were! His only friends. God! It was true. They were his only friends. The realization jarred him. He had no one else in the world to talk to, to have lunch with, to argue with, to like or dislike. Everyone else on earth was an alien stranger. These three wandering vagrants were the sum total of his entire life.

'Joe.' Maxie poked his arm with her finger. 'Come back.'

'I wish I could,' he said.

'What room are you in?'

'I haven't even checked in yet.'

'Don't bother. Move in with me. I'm in 232.'

'Okay.' He thought about it. 232. That was on

the second floor. Not too high up. In an emergency, he could always climb down a drainpipe or something.

They all went to the track together.

A horse named Crimewave won the first race. Roscoe knew the owner and they'd all bet on him. Except Milch. He knew the jockey riding Junk Dealer and risked four hundred on him. And lost.

'That's the s-s-s-story of my life,' he hissed, sobering up. 'The jock's a f-f-fag. He wears p-pantyhose. I got news for you, sh-shithead. Come 'ere.'

He led Joe behind a stairway, sweaty with excitement.

'I sewer again,' he whispered.

'What?'

'The blonde!' He pulled out a flask, took a swig. 'I sewer again.'

'You told me. In Berkeley.'

'N-n-n-no! Right here in Louisville. Yesterday at the airport.'

Joe began to sweat too. He thought he was going to black-out. Dots and flashes invaded his eyes. He wiped them away.

'Did she say anything, Milch?'

'Yup, we talked about you. She said you might be comin here ...' He belched. 'She said you was in Wheeling last week and won ten big ones. Is it true?'

'Yeah.'

'You lucky prick! I want twenty-five percent. Otherwise I'll tell her where you are. She gave me another number to call.'

With an effort, Joe forced all his muscles to relax. She

didn't know he was in Louisville. She said he might be coming here. So she wasn't sure. There was time to lose her. All he had to do was stall greedy Milch.

'Right,' he said. 'Twenty-five percent. You got a deal. Meet me at the hotel tonight. Maxie's room. 232.'

'Joe!' Maxie found them. 'Come on! Hurry up! Roscoe says there's a sure thing in the next race. A horse called Morgan.'

46

He escaped during the third race and took a taxi to Standiford.

'How'd Morgan do?' the driver asked.

'He won,' Joe told him.

'No shit? Way to go! I bet ten bucks on him. My wife heard Little Orphan Annie singing "Tomorrow Tomorrow" on the radio and she says, "Hey! That's a sign! There's a horse in the second race named Morgan." "So what?" I ask her. "Morgan means tomorrow in German," she says. So I said what the hell. Give it a shot. Five to one.'

Joe glanced out the rear window. There was another taxi just behind them.

Who's there? Is that you, Sergeant?

No, sir. Corporal of the guard.

Where's the Sergeant, Corporal?

He's gone, Lieutenant.

Gone where? I have to talk to him.

I think he deserted, sir.

Deserted? That's impossible! Why would he desert?

He said he was tired of your bullshit. He wanted to go home. We all do, the whole troop. We've had enough of this fucking around.

You're insubordinate, soldier. Stand at attention when I'm talking to you.

Up your ass!

The other taxi followed them for three blocks, then turned into the Coliseum. He watched the streets. He saw blonds everywhere – standing at bus stops, sitting on benches, walking on the pavements, shopping in the malls, parking their cars. How had she found out he'd been in Wheeling Downs and won ten grand?

'That's my old lady all over,' the driver was saying. 'She reads her horrorscope every day in the papers. If it's a bad day, she just stays home. Won't leave the house. "Let's go bowling," I tell her. "No way," she says, "my horrorscope says don't take no unnecessary risks."'

At the airport, Joe walked around the terminal lot, checking the signs on the parked buses. 'Radcliff,' 'New Albany,' 'Bardstown,' 'St. Matthews.' He found a mini-shuttle going to Lexington and climbed aboard.

He still had his old 4 Straight 'Royal Golden' card in his belt. It entitled a crowned king to honorary status in any private gambling club in the country. There was a Syndicate casino somewhere in Lexington. If he could find it, and if they'd let him in, he'd be safe there – for how long? A while. At least until tomorrow.

For five dollars a bum led him to the building. It was on High Street, a sandstone blockhouse with a bronze front door. In the vestibule, a blowsy-faced hood in a dinner jacket took the card and picked up the phone.

'Please wait,' he said.

'A hard place to get into.' Joe prayed to be admitted,

to have that big bronze barricade close behind him, snugly isolating him from the outside world.

'We're selective.' Blowsy-Face handed back the card. 'It's the only way to keep the riffraff out.'

An inner door opened, another dinner jacket appeared, beckoning. Joe followed him inside.

He immediately felt sheltered. The walls were all marble and glass, the carpets like dark grass, the lights subdued, the shadows protective.

A waiter asked him if he wanted a drink. He ordered an Irish whisky.

In the front of the room, under lamps, were several blackjack games. The bankers were all girls in blue jeans and sweaters.

Farther on, under a spotlight, was a roulette table. The croupier was a braless Japanese girl wearing an open leather vest and tights, a monocle in her eye.

In the back, miles away, was a poker enclave, enclosed in a colonade of stainless steel poles.

And best of all, off to one side, was an emergency exit.

He sank into a deep couch and sipped his drink. He felt more and more secure. The place was a bunker. Fort Invincible. She'd never get in here. He'd stay until they closed, if they ever closed.

But he missed the sergeant.

Corporal!

What do you want, Lieutenant?

Send out a patrol. Five men. Bring him back.

Forget it, man. They'd never find him. They'd just desert too. Sooner or later everybody'll be gone. Then what will you do? Fort Invincible! Hah! hah! hah! You gotta be kidding! What's the date?

A man in a scarlet jacket was sitting beside him, filling out a check. 'Did I wake you? Sorry. What's the date?'

'The twenty-third.'

'Not any more. It's twelve-thirty. Tomorrow. The twenty-fourth.'

'Oh right.'

He got up and walked over to the roulette table. He bought some hundred dollar chips and smiled at the Japanese croupier.

'How many times has the black come up in the last hour?' he asked her.

She scowled at him, her monocle blazing in the spotlight. 'Fifteen times, sir.'

'Ah hah! That's what I've been waiting for!' He put all his chips on the red. And won.

The other players gazed at him, intrigued.

'It never fails,' he told them. He gathered up his winnings and moved on to the blackjack games.

The fellow in the scarlet jacket was there, looking haggard and frantic, darting from one table to another, playing wherever there was an opening.

Joe watched the punters. They were young, ravishing, alert. He saw one of them wink at a passing waiter. Why did he always see things no one else saw? Why was he always *watching?*

He ordered another drink.

He was fully at home here now. He began giving names to the people around him, as if they were horses at the track. Scarlet Jacket, Fatass, Shorty, Big Boobs, Hog Face, El Creepo, Dashing Playboy, Frankenstein.

That had been a mistake, going to all those races. A fatal error. That's how she'd found him. He'd established a pattern. He'd have to make a clean break now. Switch channels. There were clubs like this everywhere. Secret, secluded, 'highly selective.' He knew of one in Topeka, Kansas, another in Augusta, Maine, two of them in Baltimore, another in Minneapolis. His gold card could get him into any of them. He'd make a grand tour, visit them all, one after the other, state by state …

No … hold it. That would only be establishing another pattern. Sooner or later she'd intercept him. He had to be more unpredictable than that.

Maybe he'd buy a backpack and a tent and go camping in Montana. There were forests there, endless forests, trees higher than the Eiffel Tower. He'd fly to Great Falls tomorrow – today – then hike up into the Rocky Mountains and sleep on the banks of the Flathead River and the Bitterroot and …

Shit.

He didn't feel like playing blackjack. He wandered into the enclave and watched the poker games. What the fuck was he doing here anyway? Chicago. That's where he should go. Population 4,000,000. He'd be just one more non-person in the multitude. He'd rent a loft and write a book. A novel. No, not a novel. A treatise, a thesis, a monograph. On poker. No, on Hannibal. Why hadn't he marched to Rome after his victory at Cannes? Maharbal asked him, 'So what now, boss?' And Hannibal replied, 'I'll think it over.' Here was a general who'd just defeated two enemy armies and instead of winning the war he just climbed on his elephant and went sightseeing. Why?

'I don't know,' Joe said.

Scarlet Jacket passed him. He stopped, turned.

'Beg pardon?'

'I was just wondering ... uhh when this place closed.'

'Five p.m.'

'Thanks.'

So he didn't have all night after all. It was three o'clock. He had two hours to figure out something. To come to a decision, to get off his ass.

He had to take a leak.

He went into the men's room. It was a long, dim, marble vault lined with sinks and booths.

He was washing his hands when he heard a muffled shot. *Pocoom.*

He knew instantly what it was. It usually only happened in old movies about Monte Carlo. The ruined nobleman loses everything at the *chemin-de-fer* tables, then comes strolling out of the casino and stands for a moment on the terrace staring at the Mediterranean. He takes a tiny pearl-handled revolver from his pocket ...

Now it had happened for real.

He ran over to the last booth, opened the door. A man was sitting on the floor holding a .32. His face was gone.

Joe turned away, sickened. Then he saw the scarlet jacket hanging on the inside of the door.

So simple! He pulled off his own coat, hung it open. Simple and foolproof. No face. It would be – what? – two or three days before they identified him. Time enough to be long gone. Meanwhile, Joe Egan had bid this world goodnight. He took down the scarlet jacket, pulled it on. A size too large. No matter.

He closed the booth and went back out into the casino.

He stopped at the colonnade, glanced at the clock on the wall. 3.10. Did Scarlet smoke? He searched his pockets, found a silver cigarette case filled with Fine 120s. He lit one. In another pocket was a pair of dark glasses. And a Jaguar keyring. A car! Jesus! A Jag! This was too good to be true. Goodbye, Kentucky.

He donned the glasses, started across the room to the exit.

He saw her just in time.

She was standing on the rim of the crowd around the roulette table, watching the spinning wheel.

'*Vingt noir,*' the croupier sang. '*Pair et passe.*'

47

He retreated quickly into the poker enclave, opened the first door he saw. It was a dining room, closed at this hour, the chairs on the tables, no one in sight. He ran through a passage into the kitchen, as dark as a crypt. He unbolted a back door, pulled it open. An alley. And, around the rear corner of the sandstone building, the parking lot. He found Scarlet's XJ6C, unlocked it, slid behind the wheel, turned the key in the ignition. The motor hummed. He drove out to High Street.

He passed Idle Hour, then he was on Todds Road. At five o'clock he was in Boonesboro.

The roads were deserted, the morning hot and thick. The sky turned watery green, shrouding the landscape in smoky rolling lava.

Two cops on motorcycles passed him, heading north.

He grinned at them and saluted. They both nodded gravely, as solemn as Supreme Court judges.

He passed an elderly farmer sitting on a fence like a buzzard. He saluted him too. The old man gave him the finger.

Six o'clock.

He switched on the radio.

'... died of a self-inflicted handgun wound. The victim has been identified as Joseph Egan, of Santa Monica, California.'

There it was. Now he was somebody else. Good enough.

He pulled a wallet out of the pocket of his scarlet jacket, read his new name on the driver's license and credit cards. *James* W. *Payne.*

He began Chapter I of his autobiography.

'Payne is an alias. My father was a Nazi war criminal. His real name was Wolfgang-Ludwig von Unglück and he was an SS *Gruppenführer* during WW2, responsible for the extermination of untold thousands of innocent martyrs. He escaped to America in 1945 and married my mother, a Southern Belle from Gum Sulphur, Kentucky. At the age of eleven she eloped to New Orleans with a hunchbacked mulatto who was the beekeeper on the family plantation

How had she gotten into the club? Could she turn herself into a puff of mist, like a vampire, and drift through the keyholes of bronze doors and cracks in sandstone walls? If not even a locked dungeon could keep her out, then he wasn't safe from her anywhere. He'd stay in the open from now on, he'd never stop moving. Never.

But not too fast. He slowed to 55. He didn't want to be stopped for speeding. That reminded him of something ... what? what? Yes. Making love to Iraq in the room with the headlines on the walls. 'Slow down,' she'd told him, 'or you'll be arrested for speeding.' No, wait. The headlines on the wallpaper ...

that was Maxie's bedroom in Indianapolis … no … in Vegas …

God! His dull brain was wrought with things forgotten. How much of *Macbeth* did he remember?

Thou sure and firm-set earth
Hear not my steps which way they walk
For fear the very stones prate of
My whereabouts.

He needed gas.

'Where yuh headin?' the mechanic asked him. He was a lean, tough, tattooed hick in greasy overalls, his squirrel eyes examining every inch of the Jag as he filled the tank.

'Nowhere in particular.'

'That's where I always wanted to go' – giggle – 'but I can never find it.'

'Am I still in Kentucky?'

'Hell yeah! Where'd yuh think yuh was at' – snigger snigger – 'Soody Arabia? A feller's gotta be pretty damn dumb not to recognize Kentucky when he's sittin right here in the middle o' it. Nice car' – giggle – snigger – 'where you steal it?'

'Where does that go?' Joe pointed to a back road on the other side of the gas station.

'Place called Wolf Coal. But twix here and there ain't nothin but backwoods. Get lost in there they'll never find yuh.'

'That'll be just peach with me.'

'You talk funny. Where you from?'

'The land of lost content.'

The road climbed over low hills between dusty fields and broken fences, then entered ten miles of dense woods.

It began to rain.

'In just a moment,' the radio said, 'the curtain will rise on the last act. We're in a bridal chamber. The chorus sings a wedding song. "Noble couple, love awaits you in this nook …"'

Joe switched it off, turned on the wipers.

Just ahead of him a rickety plank bridge crossed a creek. On the edge of the trees, blocking the road, a car was parked, covered with a tarpaulin.

He slowed to 30 … 20 … 10 … pulled to a stop behind it.

He sat staring at it, rattled. It looked like a bloated wet bundle. The rain, splashing down on the canvas, glittered like melting gems.

He drove around it, his left wheels spinning on the muddy brink of a ditch.

He accelerated, crossed the bridge.

Farther on, three roads forked. In a field to the right was a sagging barn. He drove behind it, stopped, jumped out of the Jag. He ran back to the fork.

The rain faded, the sun glowed through the trees.

The road to the bridge stretched before him, as straight and empty as a runway.

He waited, hoping that all his instincts were faulty, that this sudden dread was just his usual paranoia.

Then he heard the distant hum-hum-hum of an approaching car. A mere whisper at first, then a powerful growling drone, louder and louder.

The bundle of tarpaulin appeared. He stepped into the bushes. It came toward him, its canvas sheath puffing and flapping in the wind.

It thundered past, roaring away into the top of the fork.

He ran across the field to the barn, climbed into the Jag.

He drove back to the bridge. The lid on Lacuna Pit was loose, monstrosities were squeezing out from under it, rising all around him. Hysteria sat in the back seat, tapping him on the shoulder.

He hit the brakes, skidding wildly, the tires howling and squealing.

The bridge was on fire, flaming like a pyre.

48

There wasn't room enough to turn. He put the Jag in reverse, backed all the way to the fork, swung to the right, sped past the barn.

He slid to a stop. A log was lying across the road. He reversed again, backed to the fork again, spun around, took the left turn.

He was in a daze. That wouldn't do. He wasn't being – what was the word? – *retentive.* That wouldn't do either. This was no time to be stupefied.

Okay.

He closed the Pit's lid firmly, searched for his cigars. He didn't have any. They were in the other jacket. He lit a Fine 120.

First of all, he had to make sense out of these fucking roads. Going back the way he came was impossible. Okay. So he had to go forward. Or sideways. Or somewhere.

He passed a pond, a swamp, a smashed billboard. '... *SHOPPING DAYS TILL CHRISTMAS!*' More ponds. Three or four of them.

Okay. He was looking for a signpost, or some yokel to tell him where he was and how to get out of here. *Main highway's just down thataway a spell, just keep goin past Paw Moonshine's still and KKK Hq till you come to a statue of ole Stonewall Jackson covered with birdshit ...*

But there was no one. Nothing.

He drove through a tunnel of thickets growing above the road. He passed the ruins of a church, then a clearing that was once a baseball diamond. Vines covered the bleachers, a gutted tractor was in the middle of the field.

Did he have a head-start? Maybe. She hadn't seen him, he was certain of that. If he could only get on a freeway, he could be in Tennessee by tonight. Or Missouri or Arkansas.

A freeway! A freeway! My kingdom for a freeway!

The road curved down to a river – or was it the creek again? Or another pond? He drove along the winding bank.

The tarpaulin-covered car blew its horn at him.

He looked back, startled.

It was on the opposite bank, speeding after him, coming abreast of him.

They rolled along together, side by side, the tan rocky water between them.

Okay. What was he supposed to do now? An unidentified object, all wrapped up like a package, was chasing him through never-never land. What about it? Joe? Are you awake? Look alive!

The windshield was swarming with tiny whirling curlicues of light. (That was his augmenting blood pressure. He should be wearing one of Maxie's patches!)

The bundle on the other bank blew its horn again. *Boooop booooop booooop!*

Then the road looped away from the river and climbed into more woods.

He was doing 70. The miles and trees flew past the windows.

The curlicues evaporated. He suddenly felt better. He was on the move. That's all that mattered. He was running. That's what he did best. Okay. He'd walked stupidly into another trap. She hadn't come to the casino for him. She hadn't even known he was there. She'd been looking for Scarlet Jim Payne. Joe Egan's suicide must have puzzled her for a while, then she'd probably just shrugged and said, one or the other, or both, they're contrapuntals. (That was a word he hadn't used for a long long time!) Jim or Joe. Heads or tails.

Well, he'd just have to untrap himself.

Hey!

Up ahead, on the turning of a sharp bend, was a mailbox!

It looked so real! So tangible! Maybe he wasn't in dreamland after all!

He pulled up beside it.

Leaning against it was a scythe.

He drove on.

She was laughing at him. Playing with him. The whirling curlicues swarmed back into the windshield. *Good afternoon, Joe. Behold, all flesh is as the grass and lo! the grass withers and the flower decays. Remember?*

I remember. All my other thoughts but that are buried. Everything else is lost and gone.

Well, what of it? She still hadn't caught him. She could stick her scythe up her ass.

Another bend in the road and there was the tarpaulin bundle, parked in the middle of a beanfield. Four kids were pulling off the canvas.

It was a dented old Buick. Painted on its sides were the words *'DESTROY!'* and *'HARD ROCK'* and *'FUCK!'*

They waved to him as he passed.

49

Well, so much for that. False alarm.

She wasn't kidding around, *he* was. He'd been playing games with himself. Cowardly, self-indulgent, tiptoeing-past-the-graveyard games. Running amuck like a steer in a thunderstorm. Whirling curlicues indeed! It served him right. Paranoia was one thing, drivelling cringing gutlessness was another. He was in worse shape than he thought.

Sleep. He had to sleep. Get out of this jungle and find a motel and …

Anyway, he could loosen up now. Think calm thoughts. Enjoy the scenery. What scenery?

He was driving past more fields with broken fences, through more woods and swamps. The heavy air smelled of sap and tar.

He switched on the radio.

'… fingerprints found on the door of the lavatory where James Payne allegedly shot himself have been identified as belonging to the same Joseph Egan, a fugitive from justice, wanted for murder in the state of Florida. He is believed to be still in the Kentucky area, driving the victim's car, a Jaguar XJ6C, license plate number …

Oh, brother! Not that again! Florida! Murder! Jesus! Now he was really in trouble. This was really panic-button time. That bumpkin at the gas station would remember him. So would those two cops on motorcycles …

The engine stalled. The windows oozed with gurgling slime.

He opened the door, jumped out.

The front wheels were submerged in a bog. Now the hood sank too. So did he. He was up to his knees in the gluey mud.

He lunged to the back of the car, remembering Chubby in Raleigh … wading … going under …

Plodding in the hungry suction, losing both his shoes, he climbed up to the road.

The Jag's rear wheels rose into the air as the front end slipped deeper into the mire, vertically, down … down … gulp!

The radio was still playing. A country singer was yodeling

Ooooo do not long for yesterday
For yesterday is gone
Gone far away
And gone forever and forever
And forever and a day …

Well, this was great. He sat down on the hot tar. Just great. No shoes.

Flies buzzed around his face. He brushed them away.

No car either. Nifty.

He heard a loud *click-click-click-click* behind him, like a Spanish dancer's castanets.

Three rattlesnakes were uncoiling on a rock, gliding down to the road, spitting and hissing angrily, zooming in on him.

Hey! The whole family! Mom and Dad and Junior!

The first struck him on the foot, the other on the thigh, the third on the hip.

Howdy, Lieutenant!

Sergeant! You've come back!

You lost your boots, sir.

Yes, I ... I got stuck in the mud. I'm glad to see you!

I wanted to say goodbye, sir.

Goodbye? You're leaving again?

Not me, Lieutenant. You.

Me? I'm not going anywhere.

Yes, you are, sir. You see, it's an old tradition in this regiment. When the commander is bit by three rattlesnakes, he's discharged.

Are you trying to be funny?

So long, Lieutenant. I'm mighty proud, sir, to have went campaigning with you, fighting Apaches and all that. Even though, I gotta tell you, most of the time I didn't know what was going on.

Wait a second, Sergeant! Don't go!

Enough of this nonsense. What was he doing? Look at this. Sitting on his ass in the middle of hell, raving.

Had he really been bitten by three fucking rattlesnakes – *three* of them! – or had he only imagined that?

He tasted brass in his mouth, as if he'd been sucking pennies.

Would he end up as a headline on the wallpaper? *'Gibbering Lunatic Perishes in Kentucky!'*

Well, he got what he deserved. He never should have taken this back road to nowhere.

The hot air scalded him. He couldn't inhale. His nose was bleeding.

He still missed that cat ... what was his name? Emile.

The flies were back, buzzing all around him. Reading the menu.

Oh shit!

Here she is.

She came across the nearby field, walking unhurriedly out of the setting sun, taking her time. She looked like a pretty blond milkmaid, strolling through a meadow of a pastoral. He crawled across the road to a fence, pulled himself to his feet. *Ho! ho! ho! Just go Joe go go go! She'll get you if you go too slow.*

He stumbled down a slope covered with dandelions.

There was still time. She hadn't seen him yet. He'd hide in the trees over there, not making a sound. And when she was gone, he'd go back ... back ... back ... all the way to the lake ... to his eleventh birthday ... and instead of walking along Greenwood Avenue, he'd take another street to school ... hold it! Hannibal! He suddenly realized why Hannibal had never captured Rome. The simplicity of the explanation dazzled him. It was so obvious! It was because … because … But the thought lasted only an instant… then it was gone … gone … Fuck Hannibal!

'Let us pray,' Father Patrick said. 'Hail, Holy Queen, Mother of Mercy, our life and our hope. To thee we cry, poor banished children of Eve …'

Hey! He wasn't moving! He was standing still! His feet were frozen, his knees numb. He was going to fall.

'To thee do we send up our sighs, mourning and weeping in this valley of tears …'

Will somebody please tell that priest to shut up!

He managed to turn around without toppling over.

She was just behind him, coming down the slope through the dandelions. Her purple eyes were flickering. She was smiling, radiant with glee.

What now? What was he supposed to do? Where was his old coign of … what did they call it? Coign of … Maybe he could fake it! Was that possible? Play possum. Could he do that?

She stood before him.

He'd never been *this* close to her.

A dog was barking somewhere in the woods. Then a bell tolled.

Could he fake it? Could he?

She put her hands on her hips, tilted her head, studied him.

It was raining again.

She still hadn't changed … not after all these years … still the same … exactly the same …

She was laughing now, reaching for him, coming closer … closer … closer …

He'd try to fake it, yeah. What else could he do?

She took him in her arms.

The kids in the Buick found him later that evening, lying in the grass beside the road.

His leg was swollen, his lips were black, he was as rigid as a corpse.

But he was still alive.

Also published by Dover Publications

Keep reading for an extract from ...

'One of the most remarkable combinations of a private-eye novel and psychological suspense story, with an entirely new slant, that has ever been published.'
The New York Times Book Review

'A pivotal work in the history of mystery fiction.'
Maxim Jablowski, *Guardian*

1

The Eye's desk was in a corner by the window. Its single drawer contained his sewing kit, his razor, his pens and pencils, his .45, two clips of cartridges, a paperback of crossword puzzles, his passport, a tube of glue, a tiny unopened bottle of Old Smuggler scotch, and a photo of his daughter.

The window overlooked a parking lot two floors below. There were eleven other desks in the office. It was nine thirty.

He was sewing a button on his jacket and watching the lot, where an old guy in overalls was rifling a yellow Toyota. The bastard seemed to have keys fitting all the cars and had already hit a Monza V8, a Citroen DS, and a Mustang II. He took a carton of cigarettes out of the yellow Toyota now, closed and relocked the door. Nobody could see him from the street because he was crawling on his hands and knees. He scampered over to a Jag XJ6C.

The Eye dropped the sewing kit into the drawer, pulled on his jacket, picked up the phone, and called the basement. A few minutes later three thugs from the guards' squad closed in on the thief. They took his booty and the keys away from him, dumped a bucket of water over his head, and threw him out of the lot.

It was ten o'clock.

The Eye did the last four crosswords in the paperback, finishing the book. He tossed it into the wastepaper basket.

At ten thirty he borrowed *Le Figaro* from the girl sitting at desk eight, read the headlines, the *Cornet du jour,* the Vincennes racing results, and the *Programmes radiotélévision.* He tried to do the French *mots croisés* but gave it up.

The young swinger at desk nine passed him *Playboy,* and he looked at the nudes. All the girls were lying askew, playing with themselves slyly. *'MISS AUGUST, far-out Peg Magee (left) is turned on by Arab movies, skin diving, Mahler, and zoology.' 'MISS DECEMBER, demure Hope Korngold (right), admits her erotic fantasies often involve subways, buses, and ferryboats. All aboard!'*

He watched the parking lot again for a while. Then, at eleven thirty, he took the photo out of the drawer and studied it. He usually did this for a half-hour or so every morning he was in the office.

It was a group shot of fifteen little girls sitting at tables in a classroom. His wife sent it to him in sixty-one, in a letter postmarked Washington, D.C. *'Here's your fucking daughter, asshole! I bet you don't even recognize her, you prick! P.S. Fuck you!'*

It was true – he had no idea which of the children was Maggie. He'd flown to Washington and spent two months looking for them, but there had been no trace of them there. Watchmen bureaus all over the country tried for ten years to locate them, then had just put the file away in the dead archives.

He set the photo against the telephone on the desk, leaned back in his chair, and crossed his arms.

Fifteen little girls with camera-shy faces. Seven- or eight- or nine-year-olds. One of them was his daughter. She would be twenty-four years old this July.

His favorite for a long time had been the uncombed moppet in the white sweater sitting under a crucifix hanging on the wall. She was holding an apple and scowling. Then he'd switched to the blonde with the ponytail sitting by the blackboard at the opposite side of the room. She was biting a pencil. On the board was neatly chalked the beginning of Psalm 23: *'The Lord is my shepherd, I ...'* Then, for years, his choice had lingered on the pale narrow visage with the bangs in the last row. Her hands were tightly clasped and she looked terrified. Then the girl next to her had attracted his fancy. She wore glasses and was grinning ...

But he no longer had any preferences. He knew them all by heart now and loved every one of them.

The classroom was the most familiar decor of his life: three walls, crucifix, tables, blackboard, the psalm, the apple. And the fifteen lovely faces, like infantile mug shots, the myriad of gazing eyes ... and in the far corner a door through which he knew he would one day enter and call her name. And out of the multitude would rise his lost child.

He was absolutely certain of this.

He stared through the window. The old man in the

overalls was back in the parking lot, looting the glove compartment of a Thunderbird.

The telephone rang. It was Miss Dome, Baker's secretary, summoning him upstairs.

It was noon.

Watchmen, Inc., filled two basement levels and the second, third, and fourth floors of the Carlyle Tower. Baker's office was in the northeastern corner of the fourth floor, an enormous salon with two Van Goghs, three Picassos, and a Braque covering one entire wall.

Baker was only twenty-nine years old. He had inherited the agency from his father a year ago. The old-timers downstairs ran the business, but he always handled what he called 'the thousand-dollars-a-day clients' himself.

Two of them, an elderly man and woman, both in tweeds, were sitting in Hepplewhite chairs facing the refectory desk. Baker introduced them to the Eye: Mr. and Mrs. Hugo.

The Eye knew the name. Hugo shoe stores. Old-fashioned 'booteries' (Founded in 1867) on downtown streets in all the big cities. He remained standing and tried to anticipate the squeal. A family problem, surely. A son or a daughter straying off the beaten track.

He was right.

Baker struck a pose, looking grave and professional. 'Mr. and Mrs. Hugo have a son,' he announced. 'Paul. He graduated from college recently and is unemployed for the moment.'

Mr. Hugo laughed nervously. 'He's been unemployed for the last ten months!'

'He's made no effort at all to find a job,' Mrs. Hugo said. 'He's just loafing.'

'He has a girlfriend,' Baker continued. 'His parents want to find out something about her. They want to know just how deeply the boy is involved. You follow me?'

The Eye nodded. A college boy and a hustler. Dad and Ma desperate. A big retainer. He turned to Mr. Hugo. 'What's the girl's name, sir?'

Mr. Hugo twitched. 'We don't know. We've never met the young lady.'

'She's been calling him up at the house,' Mrs. Hugo whined. 'That's how we found out about her.'

Baker emerged from his chair, ending the session (he had a squash date at the Harvard Club at one). 'Establishing her identity won't be any problem,' he said. And he walked around the desk and stood staring at the front of the Eye's jacket. 'They would like a preliminary report within twenty-four hours. Is that possible?'

'Yes.' He fingered his buttonhole. The goddamned button was gone!

'Can we hear from you this time tomorrow?'

'Yes.'

'That's all, then. Thank you.'

The Eye bowed to Mr. and Mrs. Hugo and left the office. He wondered where the hell the button was. He found it out in the corridor, on the floor by the elevators.

On his last assignment he'd followed an embezzler named Moe Grander to Cheyenne, Wyoming. (The guys downstairs called him 'Grander the Absconder.')

He'd cornered the Eye in an alley one night and tried to brain him with a hammer. The Eye had shot him in the stomach. Watchmen, Inc., did not approve of killing suspects, and he'd been confined to his desk ever since. The Hugo job meant that the interdiction was lifted. The idea of escaping from the Tower and going out on the streets again elated him. He decided to skip lunch.

He took his sewing kit from his drawer and checked a Minolta camera out of the supply room. He went down to the second basement and asked the motor pool girl if he could have a car. She gave him the keys to the yellow Toyota.

He went out to the parking lot. The old thief in the overalls was still there, but scurried off when he saw the Eye coming.

It was a quarter to one. The sky was like greasy golden dishwater, the air tasted of hope and glee, the glittering windows of the Tower almost blinded him.

He climbed into the yellow Toyota and drove across the city.

MARC BEHM was born in 1925 in Trenton, New Jersey, and served with the US Army in Europe during the Second World War. After playing a variety of small parts in American television, he eventually made a name for himself as a screenwriter. When he retired from screenwriting, he published a number of novels, including *Afraid to Death* and *The Eye of the Beholder*, both now published by Dover Publications, Inc.